The jarring memory of Travis Rafferty's hoarse voice resonated in her mind.

Finding people is what I do best.

A cold chill snaked down Meredith's spine. She reined her horse around, suddenly anxious to be home. She'd made the journey to her house hundreds of times, on far worse evenings. Still, a knot clenched in the pit of her stomach.

Finding people is what I do best, Angel.

For months after the escape, she'd awakened in the middle of the night, her heart exploding in her chest, half expecting to see Rafferty standing there, looming over her. Even after she'd moved to Texas, the dreams had persisted.

She nudged her heels into her horse, goading him into a faster pace. An eerie feeling that someone watched her prickled her skin. She searched the road ahead, looking for any sign of danger. Tense seconds passed without incident and she started to feel a little foolish.

"Stop borrowing trouble, Meredith," she said to herself.

MARY BURTON

RAFFERTY'S BRIDE

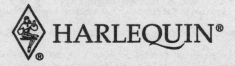

HARLEQUIN®

TORONTO • NEW YORK • LONDON
AMSTERDAM • PARIS • SYDNEY • HAMBURG
STOCKHOLM • ATHENS • TOKYO • MILAN • MADRID
PRAGUE • WARSAW • BUDAPEST • AUCKLAND

ISBN 0-373-29232-5

RAFFERTY'S BRIDE

Copyright © 2002 by Mary Taylor Burton

Visit us at www.eHarlequin.com

Printed in U.S.A.

Please address questions and book requests to:
Harlequin Reader Service
U.S.: 3010 Walden Ave., P.O. Box 1325, Buffalo, NY 14269
Canadian: P.O. Box 609, Fort Erie, Ont. L2A 5X3

For my sister, Kim

Prologue

Libby Prison
Richmond, Virginia
February 1864

As a boy, Travis Rafferty had never been the best thief in Richmond's back alleys, but for a time, he'd managed.

Until the day he'd failed to outrun the sheriff.

As the lawman had hauled fourteen-year-old Travis to the army post, he'd told him the service was just what he needed. The military would give Travis direction, a sense of honor, and would teach him patience, whether he liked it or not.

To Travis's surprise, he'd taken to the structure and discipline, not to mention the warm bed and regular meals. His keen mind, just as starved as his body, had lapped up every lesson thrown at him. He'd discovered hidden talents for scouting, marksmanship, and he'd learned to read and write.

The army became his family and molded the boy into a man.

At thirty-two, he'd risen to the rank of captain and earned the respect of his men and the brass in Washington.

The army had done a lot for Travis Rafferty.

But it had never taught him how to be a good prisoner of war.

Travis tapped his long fingers against the grimy wood floor, wishing away the next nine hours. The afternoon sun's orange-red light streamed through the half-dozen barred windows into the long, squalid cell packed with a hundred half-starved Union soldiers.

Some of his fellow prisoners of war huddled close to the water barrel, others sat in darkened corners, some lingered near the door, but each man was focused on one thought—in nine hours, they'd be free.

Since the Rebs had captured him three weeks ago, he'd been planning his escape. He and the other men had been digging a cramped tunnel that now stretched from the prison kitchen to a nearby warehouse. Tonight, once the sun set, they'd leave.

Everything had gone as he'd planned.

Almost.

The sweet taste of freedom soured when he looked down at the soldier who lay dying next to him.

Travis lifted the soiled bandage covering Lieutenant Michael Ward's inflamed wound. The young soldier flinched and groaned. The lieutenant had gotten into a scuffle with another prisoner two days ago in the prison yard. The guards had fired at the two soldiers. Ward had been wounded in the shoulder, the other man killed outright.

Dr. Ezra Carter, a Union sympathizer, had dug out the bullet from Ward's shoulder and promised to return with medicine to halt the infection. But the old man, who should have come yesterday, hadn't arrived.

Rafferty cursed.

He had little in common with Ward, but the young man was Union army. Family. And Rafferty stuck by his own kind.

Ward's eyes fluttered open, his blue eyes clouded with pain. "How's it look?"

"Better," Travis lied.

"I don't feel so good," the young man whispered.

Travis managed a crooked smile. "The doctor will be here soon with your medicine."

He winced. "I want to leave with you tonight."

Ward was too ill to crawl through the tunnel. The trip north would kill him. The medicine was his only hope now. With it, he had a fighting chance. "Let's focus on getting you better."

"I'm not getting better, Captain." Desperation crept into his voice. "The pain's worse every day, and you and the others will be gone soon. I don't want to die in this place alone."

"Hold tight. Dr. Carter will come back." This helplessness made Travis angry enough to drive his fist into a wall. "You'll be fit by week's end."

Travis leaned back against the brick wall and absently rubbed the scars on his wrist, a reminder of the shackles he'd worn during his first days as a prisoner.

Ward coughed, winced at the jarring motion. "Talk to me. Keep my mind off the pain."

"What would you like to talk about?"

Ward moistened his dry lips. "Any family?"

"The army's my family."

"No wife?"

The raw hurt returned. "There was a fiancée

once, but the long absences were too much for her. She married another man.''

''I'm sorry.''

''Don't be.'' He'd been a fool to think a society type like Isabelle could handle the sacrifices and loneliness required of a soldier's wife.

''I've a new wife, Roberta,'' Ward said, his words slurring now. ''I've got to get back to her. She's everything to me.''

''You will.''

Ward shifted his position, flinched and fell back against the pallet. He closed his eyes. ''I don't want to die in this place.''

The brick wall dug into Travis's spine. He'd seen so many men die in the past three years. ''Remember, you promised me a steak dinner when we get to Washington.''

Ward managed a weak smile. ''Right.''

A disturbance outside the cell shifted Travis's attention to the crowd around the door.

''Get back,'' the guard shouted. ''Or I ain't opening this door.''

The prisoners grumbled, shoving and rubbing shoulders as they retreated a couple of steps away from the cell door.

Travis unfolded his warrior's body to his full height of six feet, two inches. His stiff joints groaned in protest, but he stood straight, feet braced apart. "That damn well better be the doctor."

A bolt slid from the latch and seconds later the cell door opened. Instead of Dr. Castleman, a young woman stood in the doorway, clutching a large leather bag and lantern.

The dim lantern light flickered on coppery curls tied at the nape of her neck. Her black cape hugged her slender shoulders but didn't hide her petite, shapely frame.

A hush fell over the ward as every man's attention shifted to the woman. Like him, most hadn't seen a female in months. She was as unexpected as a warm summer breeze in the icy cell.

The woman's gaze brushed over the large, dingy room and the sea of emaciated prisoners staring at her. Her pale face tightened and Travis half expected her to leave.

The Confederate jailer, called Spider by the men because of his spindly legs and beady eyes, enjoyed the woman's hesitation. "Serves you right if they tear you apart. You're no better than a traitor."

The woman lifted her chin. "That'll be all. I'll let you know when I'm ready to leave."

Spider spit on the floor, stepped away and slammed the door closed. "Traitor."

The woman stood with her back pressed against the door as the dozens of men gathered in a semi-circle around her. One reached out and touched her sleeve. She moved to the right to get away but bumped into another lean, wild-eyed soldier who brushed her cheek.

"Don't do that!" she said. Her panicked voice was clear and cultured.

Travis strode through the crowd of men. "Get back. Let her breathe."

Some men glared at Travis, some complained, but all moved.

Satisfied he'd not have a riot on his hands, he turned to the woman. "Who are you?"

She met his gaze, her eyes bold and bright. "Meredith Carter, Dr. Castleman's niece."

Travis cursed. "Tell me he didn't send you to his place?"

She squared her shoulders. "Uncle Ezra is very ill. He couldn't come."

He shoved his fingers through the thick bramble of his hair. Normally he kept it closely cropped, but during the long months on the trail and weeks in prison, it had grown past his collar. "I need a doctor, not a debutante."

Her chin lifted a notch. "Well, you've got a debutante who's dug out bullets, sewn torn flesh and bandaged wounds." The Southern lilt of her clear voice didn't disguise her rising anger. "But if you'd rather I leave, I will."

A thick-necked sergeant named Murphy stepped forward, brushing past Travis. The sight of a woman was too rare to pass up. "Name's Murphy. Franklin Murphy."

She nodded but said nothing.

Murphy, anxious to stay close, added, "Don't let Captain Rafferty scare you. He's first-rate. We served together. Fact, we was captured together near Ashland a few weeks back." He grew bolder, enjoying her attention. "We lost a few men but we took a good many Rebs out before they caught us."

Her hands started to shake. "My husband is a major in the Confederate army. Last I heard, they were headed toward Ashland."

Murphy's grin vanished. "I uh…"

Travis glanced down at her left hand. A bright gold ring winked in the lantern light. The idea that she was married irritated him more than it should have. "You are married to a Reb? Your uncle supports the Union."

"He and I don't agree on everything."

The men hovered close, listening to every word of their exchange. A few grumbled their disapproval. Most were happy just to be near her.

"Why are you here?" Travis demanded.

"Because my uncle begged me. He refused to rest himself until the poultice was delivered."

"Otherwise you wouldn't have come."

She pursed her lips. "No, I would not. The Union has destroyed nearly everything I've ever cared about."

"How do I know you're not here to spy on us?" His voice was quiet, full of anger.

"I'm not here to spy," she hissed. "I've come to deliver medicine, just as I promised my uncle. When I've done my job, I'm leaving and I won't be back."

He didn't like any of this. Meredith Carter was the last thing he expected today. "I don't believe you."

Challenge sparked in her eyes. "Fine. I'll leave." She turned toward the door and raised her hand to knock to summon the guard.

Studying the delicate line of her set jaw, he considered his options. He should take the medicine she'd brought and send the woman packing. The last thing he needed was a Reb's wife snooping around hours before the breakout. But he didn't know the first thing about medicine and, Lord help him, there was something about her that made him want to trust her.

"My wounded man's over here." Without waiting for a response, he took her lantern from her and guided her through the swarm of ragged men who crowded around them.

As her black skirts brushed his legs, she tripped once on the uneven wood floor. He steadied her easily and was gifted with a whiff of her perfume. He resisted the urge to inhale the sweet, feminine scent.

When they reached Ward's flea-ridden pallet, she stared down at the injured man. The anger in her eyes vanished and the stiffness in her shoulders eased.

Without a word, she knelt on the squalid floor, unmindful of the filth staining her black skirts. Her brow knit, she laid a slender hand on Ward's head. "He's burning up."

Travis squatted next to Mrs. Carter and raised the lantern high so the ring of light dripped over Ward. "Your uncle said without the poultice the fever would kill him."

She peeled back Ward's threadbare jacket caked with blood. At once, she pressed the back of her hand to her nose as the foul odor rose.

Ward stirred and opened his eyes. His gaze was unfocused, dazed. "An angel?"

She frowned. "I'm no angel."

"You sure look like one." Ward's fogged mind drifted. "If you had wings, you could carry me out of here."

Her skirts rustled as she faced Travis. "Uncle was right about the infection," she said quietly. "The poultice will help, but under these conditions, I don't know if it will be enough to save his life." Her gaze drifted across the filthy room and the piles of soiled hay.

Travis flexed his fingers. "Do what you can for him."

Mrs. Carter nodded and removed a small burlap sack from her bag, a mortar, pestle and a corked bottle filled with water. She dumped the ingredients in the mortar and worked them together into a fine paste.

"Before I put this on, I've got to clean the wound. You and your men are going to have to hold him down."

Murphy stepped forward. "I'll help."

Travis nodded. "Murphy take his legs, I'll take his hands."

Travis handed the lantern to a nearby soldier and instructed him to hold it high. The other men crowded close as he and Murphy positioned themselves on either end of Ward. The air grew thicker, hotter.

"Go ahead," Travis ordered.

Mrs. Carter pulled a clean white cloth from her bag, poured alcohol over it, and then began to scrub the wound. Immediately Ward's eyes flew open and he cried out.

Murphy tensed. "Maybe she'd best stop. He's in agony." Several men grumbled their agreement.

Travis tightened his grip and glared at the circle of men who had closed in around them. "This needs to be done. Men back up. Give her room to work."

Mrs. Carter continued with the task, removing all traces of dirt and dead flesh. The louder Ward screamed the more her hands trembled, but she stayed on task. When she finished, the room was silent, except for Ward's moans.

The soldier, now drenched in sweat, rocked his head from side to side. *"I don't want to die here."*

Shaken, Travis patted the man on the shoulder as he sat back on his haunches. "Is that the worst of it, Mrs. Carter?"

"Yes. The rest won't be nearly as bad." Shadows from the buttery light accentuated the circles under Mrs. Carter's eyes. She looked fragile, bone weary, but she was a pretty little thing.

If only they'd met in another time and place, before she'd married... Travis tossed the idea aside. No sense wondering what would never be.

As she dipped her fingers into the pasty mixture and spread it gently on Ward's wound, Travis wiped the sweat from his brow with the back of his forearm. "That smells awful."

"How could you possibly notice in *here?*" There was challenge in the question and in her green eyes.

He shrugged, oddly amused and pleased by her grit. She wasn't afraid to stand up to him or speak her mind. He liked that.

Mrs. Carter smoothed the paste over Ward's wound, working slowly, carefully. Only after she'd applied a liberal amount did she wipe her hands clean and bandage the wound.

Travis realized she'd done an excellent job. "I underestimated you."

Her spring-green gaze lifted to his and he felt the quick trip of his pulse. They were so close he could feel the heat of her body. "I know."

Neither spoke while she packed her belongings into her doctor's bag. When she'd finished, Travis rose and held his hand out to her, a peace offering of sorts. "We got off to a bad start."

She ignored his outstretched hand and pushed herself to her feet. "No harm done."

Travis lowered his hand, annoyed. He steered the conversation back to Ward. "Will he make it?"

She emitted a sigh. "If he's treated regularly."

Travis nodded. "When will your uncle be back to check on Ward?"

"My uncle's very ill, I doubt he'll be able to visit again."

Travis hated asking for favors. "What about you?"

"I don't think it's wise I return. My husband wouldn't approve at all." She reached into her bag and pulled out salve and fresh bandages. "Here are supplies to hold you for a few days."

Travis wouldn't be here to change the bandage. "Forget for a moment that a Yankee's doing the asking," he said in a tone sharper than he'd intended. "This man needs your help."

She looked as if she'd refuse again, then she glanced at Ward. The sadness reflected in her eyes told him she was the type who couldn't turn her back on the helpless. "Much depends on the guards and how generous they're feeling. Sometimes they don't let even my uncle in.''

"But you will try," he persisted.

Several soldiers in the rear of the room started to scuffle. "Get out of my way!" one shouted. "I ain't got a look at the woman yet."

"Get back," another soldier shouted. "I ain't seen much of the angel either and I'm not giving you my spot."

The prisoners on the outer edge of the crowd, anxious to get a closer look at Mrs. Carter, started to push and shove. They were willing to fight to catch just a glimpse of her. The men's voices grew louder, angrier. He might have that riot after all.

Travis dragged his gaze from Mrs. Carter. "Don't move."

As he headed away from her, she turned her attention to Ward. "Lieutenant," she said, kneeling. "You should be feeling better soon. I have to leave, but Captain Rafferty has promised to take care of you."

Ward stirred. "Rafferty?"

She tugged his blanket up to his chin. "That's right. He'll change your bandage tomorrow. I'll return if I can."

A silent warning tickled the hair on the back of

Travis's neck. He halted and turned in time to see Ward's brow furrow. "Travis can't change the bandage. He's leaving tonight with the others."

Travis sucked in a breath through his teeth. Damn it! He started to shove his way through the men.

Mrs. Carter patted Ward on the arm. "No one's going anywhere, Lieutenant."

"They're leaving me. Escaping through the tunnel," he whimpered.

She didn't look up, but her back stiffened. "Tunnel," she whispered. "Oh, God."

He saw the color drain from her face.

She knew.

Mrs. Carter rose quickly. The circle of men around Ward had heard, as well. Their admiration for her soured to suspicion.

Keeping her gaze low, she started to push her way through the men toward the door, unmindful of the prisoners touching her or that she'd left her bag behind.

A wave of fear engulfed Travis. Mrs. Carter may have helped Ward today, but that didn't change the fact that she was married to a Reb. One word from her to the guards and weeks of digging, hoping, dreaming would evaporate.

Travis snatched up the bag and intercepted her at the door. "Forget something?"

Her face flushed crimson and she took the bag. "Thank you. I must be going."

He shifted his stance, blocking her as she tried to step around him. "Not before we talk."

She managed a feeble smile. "If it's about the lieutenant, I'll come back to check on him. Tomorrow, perhaps."

He grabbed hold of her arm. "Don't play dumb. You know now about the tunnel."

She shrieked. "Let go of me."

Several men heard the sharp pitch of her voice. They stopped arguing. They moved closer, tightening around them.

Mrs. Carter looked at the men. Her body trembled but her voice was clear. "Would one of you please tell the captain to let me go?"

Travis bared his teeth and let his gaze sear into his men. "Don't move an inch."

No man stepped forward.

Panicked green eyes locked on Travis. "I came here to help that man, not gather secrets."

Something deep inside him clenched. He didn't have the luxury of trust.

He loomed over her, using his only weapon—

his massive size—to intimidate. "Well, you stumbled right into one."

Tears puddled in her eyes. "I'm not going to tell, I swear."

His fingers bit into her arm. "How can I believe you?"

"I don't know. But I swear I won't tell."

He picked up a stray curl of hers and twirled it between his fingers. Silk. "I'm going to trust you. But don't disappoint me. Because if you do, no matter how long it takes, I'll find you. Understand?"

Numbly she nodded.

He stared at her for long, tense seconds. Several men complained as word of what happened spread among them. Quickly he directed her to the door and banged on it with his palm. "Guard! Mrs. Carter's ready to leave."

Murphy stepped forward. He looked at Mrs. Carter with longing and sadness. "Word's spreading fast. The men are desperate enough to turn on her."

"I know," he muttered.

The guard shuffled down the hallway as if he weren't in a rush to do a prisoner's bidding. The jangle of keys mingled with the scrape of his feet against the plank floor.

Travis squeezed Mrs. Carter's arm hard as the guard shoved the key into the lock. Her shallow, quick breathing stopped as she held her breath.

His lips brushed her ears. "I'm the best tracker in the Union army. Finding people is what I do best. Remember that, angel."

Seconds after midnight, the alarm bell clanged and alerted the city to the prison escape. The wind propelled the frantic yelp of barking bloodhounds, the whirl of gunfire and the screams of the prisoners who were already being rounded up by the guards.

Travis, one of the first men out of the tunnel, crouched by the muddy banks of the James River and watched the Confederate guards swarming across the flatlands.

The escape had been discovered!

A bullet sang past him and forced him forward into the river's dark waters. He hissed in a breath and waded into waist-deep, icy waters, praying the dogs would lose his scent. He stumbled on the jagged river bottom, tumbling forward into the water. The slick rocks made it difficult to stand, and by the time he'd pushed himself to his feet, the frigid water had numbed his flesh. He hugged his drenched arms around his chest.

How long it took to cross the river he couldn't say. He couldn't think beyond the next step. One foot in front of the other...

His knees wobbled with exhaustion by the time he reached the other muddy bank. Frozen to the marrow, he collapsed onto the cold, sucking mire. His lungs burned and sensation had deserted his limbs.

His exhausted, malnourished body refused his command to move and for an instant he laid his head down. He'd rest just for a minute. The seductive cold lulled him deeper toward unconsciousness. God, but he was so tired.

How had this gone so wrong?

What had happened?

And then he remembered the angel.

She had sworn to keep his secret.

And, God help him, he'd believed her.

His fingers dug into the mud. Wheezing in a lungful of air, he hauled himself up to his knees. Fury goaded him to his feet. He started to jog away from the riverbank.

If Meredith Carter had told the guards about the tunnel, Travis swore he'd not rest until he found her.

No matter how long it took.

* * *

Across town, the same alarm bell startled Meredith awake. Her heart thundered in her chest and, without hesitating, she tossed back the quilts and jumped from her chair by the cold fireplace. Her white nightgown billowed around her ankles and she hurried barefoot across the cold floor to the window of her bedroom. She pushed back the heavy velvet curtains and stared out over the tin rooftops toward the prison, located by the river.

The landscape was dark except for a handful of stars in the sky, the sliver of moon and the dozens of torches flickering like buzzing fireflies near the prison and the riverbank.

Meredith leaned her head against the icy glass and shoved out a sigh. She pressed her hand against her belly. Suddenly she felt sick and lightheaded.

The prison escape had failed.

She shoved a shaky hand through her hair. She'd kept her promise to Rafferty and guarded his secret. But something deep in her soul told her he blamed her.

Finding people is what I do best.

One day he would come after her.

Chapter One

Trail's End, Texas
April 1866

"Tarnation, Miss Meredith! When Dr. Castleman pulled my last tooth, it didn't hurt near as bad." Sheriff Fox Harper rubbed his swollen jaw, then spit into a dented tin cup. "For an itty-bitty thing, you're as strong as an ox."

Meredith laid the dental pliers next to her late uncle's medical bag and crossed to the kitchen sink. Carefully she washed her hands. "If you'd called me sooner, I could have saved you a lot of pain."

The sheriff's wife, a portly woman with white hair that glistened in the lantern light, handed her husband an ice pack. "I've been telling him for days to send for you,'' said Mrs. Harper. ''But he just wouldn't do it no matter how much I nagged. Said he was worried. Said you're not a *real* doctor.''

Crimson washed up the sheriff's angled face, making his salt-and-pepper beard look two shades whiter. ''Miss Meredith, you are a fine nurse, but facts are facts. You ain't a real doctor, not like your uncle.''

Meredith sprinkled herbs into an earthenware cup filled with water and mixed them with a spoon. She understood the sheriff's concern. Her uncle had been a great doctor and all the people in Trail's End sorely missed him. ''You are right on both counts, Sheriff Harper.''

Sheriff Harper shot his wife an I-told-you-so look and pressed the ice pack to his face.

Mrs. Harper shrugged. ''I don't care about what kind of schooling you had or didn't have. In my mind you're a sight better than some of the *real* doctors I've had the *displeasure* to meet. I only hope this new doctor the town has hired isn't a drunk.''

Ignoring his wife, the sheriff pulled his wire-rim glasses out of his front shirt pocket, put them on and peered over the rim. ''What's that you're mixing up, Meredith?''

She swirled the cup around. "Just a little potion that'll help you with the pain and swelling."

He grimaced. "I don't like medicine."

Mrs. Harper shook her head. "Men. Why is it that they all turn into children when they're sick?"

Swallowing a smile, Meredith pressed the cup into Sheriff Harper's thin fingers. You'd never know the man was one of the most feared lawmen in Texas. "Drink it, Sheriff."

He raised the cup to his nose and sniffed. "Smells awful."

Meredith grinned. "Tastes even worse."

The sheriff set the cup down. "I won't drink something that smells like week-old socks."

Mrs. Harper's brown eyes flashed as if she were ready for battle. "Fox Harper, you should be ashamed. Think of all those renegades and bank robbers you've put behind bars. What would they say if they saw the mighty Sheriff Harper whining about a little medicine?"

He folded his arms over his chest. "I'll take a shoot-out over medicine any day."

Meredith picked up the cup and held it out for him. "It really will make you feel better."

He rubbed his tongue over his teeth then winced. "I feel just fine."

His wife planted her hands on her hips. "If you don't drink every drop, you'll sleep on the back porch tonight. I won't have you up all hours of the night moaning in pain."

He took the glass. "I've hardly complained at all," he grumbled.

Mrs. Harper laughed. "That's a funny one."

The old man grimaced then reluctantly raised the cup to his lips and swallowed the brew in one gulp. Immediately his face pinched and he started to sputter. He accepted a cup of water Meredith pushed into his hand and drained it, gasping. "I think you've poisoned me, Miss Meredith!"

Chuckling, Meredith dug into her bag and pulled out a small brown sack. "You'll live to be a hundred." She handed the pouch to Mrs. Harper. "Mix a tablespoon of this into a cup of water and give it to him when he wakes in the morning."

"I'm not drinking that stuff again," Sheriff Harper said, pouting.

Mrs. Harper tucked the bag in her apron pocket. "Yes you will."

Meredith laughed, knowing the sheriff was no match for his wife. "Mrs. Harper, the medicine will make him sleepy, but he needs a good night's rest. Send word if he has any more trouble."

Mrs. Harper dug four nickels out of her pocket and pressed the coins into Meredith's hand. "The first sign of trouble and I'll send someone to get you."

Meredith dropped the coins into her bag. "Thank you."

Most of her patients bartered for her services. The system worked well for the most part, but with the new doctor coming, she'd started worrying about money. These nickels would go into the strongbox in her dresser drawer, bringing her total savings to twenty dollars and eighty-two cents.

Mrs. Harper reached for Meredith's cape and handed it to her. "We'll be expecting you for the picnic, Sunday after next," she said cheerily. "*Mr. Walker* will be joining us, as well," she prompted.

Meredith knew where this was headed. She scrambled for an excuse. Mr. Walker was owner of the dry goods and one of many men Mrs. Harper had tried to foist on the widowed Meredith in the past few months. "The Miller baby is due any day. I may not be able to make it."

Mrs. Harper waved her hand, dismissing Meredith's claim. "That baby's not due for a month. And you could stand to eat a decent meal. Oh, did I mention that Mr. Walker is a widower. You've got so much in common.''

Meredith could see the wagons circling. ''I've a mountain of laundry to tend to and I haven't cleaned my house in a month.''

''That laundry isn't going anywhere.''

The sheriff rolled his eyes. ''Careful, Miss Meredith. She'll have you wed by month's end if you're not careful.''

Meredith worked up a smile. ''Not to worry, Sheriff Harper. I've stayed a step ahead of your wife so far.''

Mrs. Harper scowled. ''Honestly, Meredith, I don't understand you. You're young, beautiful and smart to boot. There are a dozen men in this town that would marry you in a snap if you only gave them the nod, but you've ignored them all.''

''I haven't ignored them, exactly,'' Meredith said, frowning. She'd kept to herself since her uncle's death, but Mrs. Harper made her sound like a hermit.

''You have.'' She held up her hand, silencing Meredith's retort. ''And don't try to deny it. Poor George Walker has done everything but paint a sign trying to get your attention. The man would have given up on you months ago if I hadn't supplied him with a little encouragement.''

Meredith rubbed the tense muscles at the base of her head. ''Mrs. Harper, I don't want another husband.''

The old woman's frown eased. ''Meredith, I know things were hard for you in Virginia. Losing your husband in the war must have been a terrible blow, and your uncle told me how folks turned on you.''

''It wasn't so bad.'' She tried to keep her voice light.

Meredith had never intended to return to Libby Prison, but she couldn't shake the memory of the starving men. The morning after the escape, she'd gone back. Rafferty and Ward were gone, but many had remained. So she'd started to make regular visits. When her neighbors and her husband's family had gotten wind of the ongoing visits, they'd ostracized her. Her mother-in-law didn't even speak to her at James's funeral.

''You're not fooling anybody. Folks stick by each other in Trail's End. We all want to see you happy and we don't want to lose you.''

Trust still didn't come easily. ''I know.''

''It's time you started letting folks into your life again—let them take care of you. Open your heart.'' She laid her hand on Meredith's shoulder. ''The war is over. I know how you nursed your uncle through all his spells, but your uncle and husband are gone. It's time you moved on with your life. Besides, Dr. What's-His-Name arrives a week from Sunday. He'll stay at the hotel for a week or two but he'll be taking over your house by month's end. Of course, you are welcome to stay here until you find a place.''

''That's kind,'' she said absently.

She ignored the ache in her belly that always came when she thought about moving. This home she'd shared with her uncle had been the longest she'd lived anywhere.

The town owned the house Meredith had shared with her uncle. It was reserved for the town doctor. After her uncle had died, the townsfolk had let her stay on, but now that the new doctor was arriving, she'd have to find a new place to live.

''I could also rent rooms at the boardinghouse.''

''Is that all you want from life—living alone in a rented room?''

''It's only temporary.''

''Temporary has a way of becoming permanent.'' Mrs. Harper brushed a stray thread from Meredith's shoulder. ''I don't want to see you alone, spending your days just taking care of others and your nights alone in a leased room. It's time to start looking ahead. You need a family of your own."

"It's hard to think about tomorrow when the past refuses to be forgotten." Meredith had hoped the move to Texas would help her leave the war behind, help her forget the faces of the men who'd died, but it still haunted her.

"Sometimes," Mrs. Harper said softly, "you've got to do something that's good for you, even if you don't feel like it. The more you move forward, the easier it gets."

The sheriff cupped his hand to his jaw. "You best surrender now, Miss Meredith. You're fighting a losing battle when you go against my Edith."

Meredith sighed. He was right of course. And so was Mrs. Harper. The war had been over for a year. James had been dead two years in September. It was time to somehow move forward. "I'll be back in Trail's End for the picnic next Sunday, Mrs. Harper. I am looking forward to meeting the doctor, but I'm not making any promises about Mr. Walker."

Beaming, Mrs. Harper laid her hand over her heart. "Far be it from me to make anyone do something they're not comfortable with. All I ask is that you keep an open mind." She leaned closer. "You know Mr. Walker bought a fancy new buggy just big enough for two. Even has fringe around the roof. When the weather turns warm in a few weeks, it'll be perfect for rides in the country."

Laughing, Meredith squeezed Mrs. Harper's hand. "Do you ever give up?"

"No, dear."

Meredith opened the back door and savored the scent of the twilight breeze. The Harpers' back porch faced south toward the rolling grasslands now bathed in an amber glow. Meredith's brown gelding, Blue, stood tethered to a bush a half-dozen paces from the back door. When he saw Meredith, he nickered and whinnied.

Frowning, Mrs. Harper hugged her shawl around her full bosom. "Dear, why don't you spend the night? You can board your horse here, get a good night's sleep, and I'll fix you a real breakfast in the morning. Maybe we could look at the new fabrics at the dry goods tomorrow."

"It's only a half-hour ride. I'll be home by dark. And I've animals at home that need to be fed."

Mrs. Harper cocked an eyebrow. "Don't tell me you've taken in another stray?"

"A few kittens and a mother cat."

The old woman shook her head. "Meredith, you're a sucker for a lost cause."

Odd, she never thought about it, but she did seem to attract more than her share of the sick, injured and homeless animals. "Maybe."

As she headed down the porch steps, Mrs. Harper said, "At least let me fetch Mr. Walker. He would be pleased to escort you home."

"I'll be fine." Meredith crossed the backyard and reached for the reins. She tied her bag to the pommel and hoisted herself up in the saddle. She wrapped the reins around her hand. "I've ridden at night more times than I can count."

Mrs. Harper shifted her feet to ward off the cold. "Someone should worry about you. A young woman shouldn't shoulder so many responsibilities alone. You have done so much for the folks in Trail's End. You're an angel."

Angel.

The jarring memory of Travis Rafferty's hoarse voice resonated in her mind. A cold chill coiled around Meredith's spine. She reined her horse around, suddenly keen to be home.

"I'm no angel, Mrs. Harper."

"Yes, you are, dear," the older woman said

softly. She patted Meredith on the arm. "Don't forget, Sunday next at one o'clock."

Meredith nudged her heels into Blue's side. "Take care of the sheriff."

The clip-clop of the horse's hooves mingled with the evening breeze. The wind whispered promises of a storm. In the distance a dog barked.

She'd made the journey between Trail's End and her house hundreds of times on far worse evenings, and she'd never had a bit of trouble.

Still a ripple of unease rolled down her spine.

She tried to laugh off the sensation. The memory of Rafferty was enough to put anyone on edge.

For months after the escape, she'd awakened in the middle of the night, her heart exploding in her chest, half expecting to see Rafferty standing there, looming over her. Even after she and her uncle had moved to Texas, and they'd put a thousand miles between them and the past, the dreams persisted.

She nudged her heels into her horse, goading him into a faster pace. Blue's ears twitched and he champed at his bit as if he didn't appreciate the brisker clip, but he complied nonetheless.

As the sun brushed the horizon, the wind started to pick up, washing over the grass in great waves. Amber light flooded the landscape, grazing the tips of the trees. In the distance, Brook Pond glistened, reflecting the rising moon in its rippling waters. An owl hooted.

Suddenly the eerie feeling that someone was watching her prickled her skin. She searched the road ahead, looking for any sign of trouble. Anxious seconds passed. When nothing happened, she started to feel a little foolish.

She moistened her dry lips. "Stop borrowing trouble, Meredith."

Drawing in several deep breaths, she started to reason away her worries as she always did when she was nervous. "Travis Rafferty is not out there lurking in the shadows." Her saddle creaked as she leaned back. "There's been no sign of the man in two years and, chances are, he has forgotten all about you. Honestly, Meredith you are being foolish."

Despite her brave words, she didn't deny the sweet wave of relief that washed over her thirty minutes later when she reached her modest whitewashed, framed house.

The wind had picked up more, straining against the tree branches and pushing the twin rockers on her front porch back and forth. A shutter on the side of the house banged with each new gust.

She slid off Blue, lifted the reins over his head and led him to the barn. When she raised the wooden bar and opened the barn door, a droopy-eyed hound dog thumped his tail in greeting and barked at her. He jumped up and down as if he'd not seen her in months.

Surprised, Meredith patted the dog's head. "What are you doing here, Shorty? Don't tell me I locked you in the barn again." She scratched the dog between his ears. "Honestly, I'd forget my head if it weren't attached. Sorry about that, fellow."

The dog barked at her.

She laughed. "I hope you left Mama Kitty and the Three Musketeers alone. They don't understand that you just want to play."

Shorty started to howl.

"Fine. Fine. I get it. You are hungry. I'll bring some meat scraps out in a minute."

The earthy smell of hay greeted her as she lit the single lantern that hung by the barn door. Raising it high, she guided Blue to his stall. Shorty followed behind, staying close on her heels. Across the aisle from Blue's stall, a gray cat strolled toward her. Nipping at her heels were three eight-week-old kittens. Two tabby. One white.

Mama Kitty brushed Meredith's leg as she hung up the lantern and set her medical bag aside. "I know. You're hungry, too." She unfastened Blue's cinch, hefted the saddle free and draped it over the side of the stall. Removing the bridle, she rubbed down the horse then stuffed fresh hay into his feed bin before she filled his trough with water. She patted him on the side and wished him a good-night.

With her lantern and medical bag in hand, she strode out of the barn toward her house. Mama Kitty rolled on her back in the dirt, but a worried Shorty stayed on her heels. "You're mighty friendly tonight. You must really be hungry."

Her boots crunched against the gravel in time with the swoosh of her wool skirts. Tired, she climbed the three steps to the narrow front porch and reached for the knob on the front door. Shorty, anxious to get in, wedged himself between her and the door.

"Oh no you don't," she said. "The last time I let you in, you chewed up my favorite shoes. You stay out here and I'll bring your bowl out."

Persistent, the dog wouldn't move, forcing Meredith to pull him back by his rope collar. "Since when did you get so bossy?"

She slipped past the dog and closed the door.

He howled and scratched at the door. "In a minute, Shorty."

The sun had set and the single lantern did little to brighten the main room that normally felt so cheery and bright. Tonight the cabin possessed an unnatural stillness punctuated only by Shorty's howls.

The odd sense of unease returned, making her hesitate. Her hand still on the doorknob, she stared into the black room. Sometimes patients waited for her on the front porch, but none had ever ventured inside.

"Hello, is anyone here?"

No one answered.

Meredith quickly lit a second lantern and hung it by the door on a peg. Her gaze skimmed over the large braided rug that warmed the floor under a settee, her knitting bag, and a small table piled high with books. From her closed bedroom door to the sturdy cookstove on the opposite end of the cabin, everything was as she'd left it. Still the hairs on the back of her neck rose.

Annoyed at her jumpy nature, she crossed to the kitchen table and set down her bag and lantern. Turning to the stove, she stoked the embers and shoved kindling inside until they flickered to life.

As the fire crackled, a warm glow danced on the walls of the kitchen.

Hovering close to the stove's warmth, Meredith pressed her hand into the small of her back, trying to stretch out the kinks.

Shorty howled louder, prompting Meredith to turn. "Honestly, Shorty, I—"

And then she saw the man step from the shadows near the hearth.

Without thinking, she snatched up a large butcher knife. Gripping its wooden handle until her knuckles whitened, she faced her intruder.

A sharp breath hissed through her nostrils. It was the kind of startled sound made when prey faced predator.

Broad shouldered, he wore a duster that cloaked his tall, muscled frame and skimmed the top of muddied boots. A Stetson shadowed his face.

Frozen by fear, Meredith stared in horror as the man stepped into the ring of lantern light.

"Miss me, angel?" Travis Rafferty said.

Chapter Two

Meredith's heart hammered in her ears as she stared at the man who'd haunted her dreams for two years. The beard and grime of the prison was gone. His skin, now tanned, accentuated razor-sharp blue eyes. Wavy hair, as black as Satan's soul, skimmed the top of his collar.

He wore crisp pants, a white shirt and muddied black boots. He was tall, with the tough muscular body of a brawler.

Her throat tightened. "Captain Rafferty."

White teeth flashed. "You remember me. I wasn't sure if you would."

"I remember."

Captain Rafferty dropped his hat on the chair by the hearth as if staking his claim. Power, barely leashed, radiated from his body.

The knife handle felt slick in her sweaty palm. "What do you want?"

"You."

The blood drained from her face. "Why?"

His gaze pinned her. "I think you know why."

A chill shot down her spine. He blamed her for the failed prison escape. "I didn't tell the guards about the escape."

He took a step closer to her. "They were on our tail minutes after we started through the tunnel. Without us making a sound, they knew we had broken out."

"It wasn't me," she whispered.

He arched an eyebrow. "Then who?"

"Someone else tipped off the guards. But I never found out who."

"Of course not," he said. Sarcasm dripped from the words.

Fear made her queasy. "From what I remember you are a man of honor," she said, trying to reach him.

His stare was dark and menacing. The truth was she didn't know what kind of man he was. "Am I?"

"Yes. You could have hurt me then, but you didn't. You let me go."

Anger brightened his eyes. ''I don't make the same mistake twice.''

Her pulse thundering erratically, she feared there be no reasoning with him. Her best chance was to escape, get to town. Sheriff Harper would protect her.

Only twenty feet to the door.

Quickly she turned and raced to the front door. Her fingers had barely scraped the cold metal of the knob when he grabbed her, whirled her around and shoved her against the wall. He wrenched the knife from her hand and drove it into the wall above her head with such force the handle vibrated. She doubted she'd ever be able to wrestle it loose.

Tears streamed down her face as he flattened his hard body against hers. ''I've traveled a long way to see you, Meredith. You're not leaving just yet, are you?''

She willed her voice to remain steady. ''You broke into my house.''

With no hint of apology, he pinned her hands above her head. His thigh pressed between hers. ''The front door was open.''

''Get out of my house,'' she cried.

''No.''

She squirmed under his iron hold but could not

move an inch. "Go back to wherever you came from. I'm not the one you want!"

For an instant, something akin to regret flashed in his eyes. "Yes, you are."

"I didn't betray those prisoners."

Just the mention of that night seemed to stoke his temper. "Tell it to the judge."

She struggled underneath his weight. "It's the truth!"

Her denial snapped his control. He jerked her away from the wall and started toward the bedroom. She dug her heels in and tried to twist free, but he pulled her along as if she were a rag doll. He shoved her into the bedroom.

His body blocking the door, he lit a lantern. Light spilled on her cast-iron bed and puddled on her unmade sheets, twisted around a rumpled yellow patchwork quilt.

Dear Lord, he was going to rape her.

She moved away from the bed, molding her back into the corner farthest from the bed. She tried not to look at the bed, tried not to think about what was going to come next. "Please don't do this."

Surprise flickered in his gaze. His frown deepened, then he laughed mirthlessly. "Your honor is safe, Mrs. Carter. You're the last woman I'd ever want.''

She was too terrified to keep her voice steady. ''Get out of my house. Get out of my life.''

His long, callused fingers banded her arm and he pulled her toward a walnut bureau. ''You've got ten minutes to pack.''

Hideous fear pricked her senses. ''Where are we going?''

''Washington.''

''Why?''

''You're going to stand trial, Mrs. Carter.''

''On what charge?''

He yanked open a bureau drawer, scooped an armload of clothes and shoved them into her arms. ''Spying.''

She clung to the rumpled garments. ''I never spied for anyone.''

''Then why the trips to the prison camp?''

Her face paled. ''How did you know about the visits?''

''I knew.'' Rafferty leaned over her, his tall frame intimidating. ''Why the visits, Mrs. Carter?''

''To help.''

He lifted an eyebrow. ''You weren't interested in helping much that night I saw you.''

"I—I never realized how awful the prisons were. I couldn't turn my back on the men anymore."

"Right." He flashed a cynical smile. "I bet your Confederate husband approved of your spying."

"James hated my visits to the prison."

He stared at her a long moment, as if surveying every detail about her. Her mouth went dry.

"You're very convincing," he said finally.

"I'm telling the truth. Yes, I was at the prison the day your men tried to escape, but it was an unhappy coincidence. Bad luck was all."

"I'd say excellent timing."

She balled her fists tighter. "How dare you judge me? You don't know the first thing about me."

"I know a lot about you." He pulled a slim leather-bound book from his pocket, flipped through several pages. "You were born in Virginia, but your father served in the army and you moved around a lot as a child. When you were twelve, your parents died. Typhoid. That's when you went to Richmond to live with your uncle, Ezra Castleman. Your uncle was a New Yorker by birth, but his late wife was a Virginian, the reason he settled in Richmond." He turned the page. "You married James Carter in February of '64. Seven months later he was killed near Petersburg."

His catalogue of facts unnerved her.

"Did I mention that before your hasty departure from Richmond in September of '64, you and your uncle made two trips to Washington that same summer?"

"We traveled north to buy medical supplies."

"Or to trade secrets."

Fear turned to frustration. "We were humanitarians not spies."

"Humanitarian?" He shoved the book back in his pocket. "Is that what you call it?"

"Yes."

His smile didn't fool her. Reliving the past was making him madder by the moment. "It took me two weeks to get back to Union lines. I nearly died from exposure. The thought of finding you again was all that kept me going."

Lantern light shadowed his angled features. "I lay awake at night for months after the breakout. The bullets and screams of the prisoners wouldn't leave me in peace. I thought about you a thousand times those first months. I didn't want to believe you'd broken your promise or that I'd been foolish enough to believe you."

His story sliced at her heart. Like so many others, the war and its horror had scarred his soul.

"I wasn't the one who told the guards," she said.

"I've evidence." He sounded almost sad.

Confused, she shook her head. "How can there be evidence? I didn't do anything."

His jaw pulsed with anger. "Lieutenant Ward. You remember Ward?"

"He was the reason I came that night. I put a salve on his wound. He's the one who told me about the escape."

He nodded. "Good memory. He's still not regained the full use of his arm, but he's been promoted to captain. He remembered you, too. And had some very interesting things to say to me."

Her eyes narrowed. "What do you mean?"

"He'd conducted his own investigation into the foiled escape. Like me, he wanted to know who was behind it. His family is well positioned. It didn't take him long to find out you were the one who'd sold us out."

"He's wrong!"

"He showed me the testimony of the prison guard who admitted that you'd tipped him off."

Her head spun. She could feel the blood drain from her face drop by drop. "The guards and most of the people in Richmond hated me because I *helped* the prisoners. You can't believe what the guards or any of my neighbors said about me."

He shrugged. "Ward begged me to let this whole matter go. He said it was best to forget the past. But I couldn't. Too many good men died that night."

She threw the clothes on the floor. "I didn't do it."

Rafferty sighed. "That's for the judge in Washington to decide." He removed a piece of paper from his breast pocket. "I've a warrant for your arrest."

She backed away from him. "I don't care about your papers. I'm not going anywhere with you."

"I'm not asking for your permission." He tossed the warrant onto her bed. "You've got five minutes to pack."

Her bravado faltered. "There are people in this town who care about me. They won't let you drag me back to Washington."

He seemed almost bored. "I suppose they could try, but we're not going through town."

Shock and fear clashed. "What about supplies?" she stammered. "The next town is a hundred miles from here."

"I was in town earlier today. I picked up everything we'll need."

"I didn't see you in town," she challenged.

"You were in the mercantile."

"I don't believe you," she whispered.

A wicked grin tipped the corner of his mouth. "George Walker seems sweet on you."

Her throat constricted. What didn't he know about her? Like a caged animal, she scanned the room. "Mr. Walker will come after me. He wants to marry me."

"Let 'em. I've nothing to hide." He nodded at her bag. "You have four minutes to pack."

She almost choked. "What can I say that'll convince you I'm telling the truth?"

"Nothing."

Shoring up her crumbling composure, her thoughts turned back to escape. She couldn't return to Washington. Alone, with little resources, she had no way to fight the manufactured evidence stacked against her.

Somehow she'd get away from Rafferty.

Her thoughts racing, she walked woodenly to a chest at the foot of her bed, opened it and yanked out a carpetbag. She snapped it open.

Once she got outside, there'd be no time to saddle Blue.

She dropped the bag in the center of her bed, then scooped the clothes off the floor and dropped them next to the bag.

She'd run to the woods.

With trembling hands, she started to fold a blouse as she forced her racing mind to calm.

Toward the stream, to the cover of the brush along the banks.

The tension in the room was maddening. She shoved the blouse and then a skirt into the bag.

She'd go west first then double back to town.

As she rummaged through the pile of clothes on her bed, her fingers skimmed her leather-bound journal. She'd written in the journal every day during the war. Somehow, words on a page diffused the horrors she'd witnessed. She'd been unable to look at the book since she and her uncle had moved to Texas.

She nearly tossed the book aside when it struck her it was the evidence she needed. She whirled and thrust the book toward Rafferty. "Read this!"

He took the book and leafed through the pages. "Your journal?"

"Yes! I wrote detailed accounts of what I did almost every day. There's no mention of spying in there."

He handed it back to her. "You're smart, Meredith, I'd never deny that. You'd never be fool enough to put your deeds on paper.''

His calmness, more maddening than threats, snapped her temper. "You don't *want* to find anything that will clear my name."

"Not true."

She slammed the book down on the bed. "You want me punished—no matter what. You're no better than a lawless vigilante."

His eyes narrowed. "I'm doing this *legally* with warrants and evidence."

She raised her fist to him. "Don't fool yourself or me. I'll bet it's easy to get a warrant against a Southerner. Emotions still run hot and there's a lot of hate and resentment toward the South in Washington."

A crooked smile twisted his lips. "As a matter of fact, it wasn't easy. No one cared about you or your spying until I forced the issue. There were plenty who told me to drop this, to walk away, but I refused. I've called in every favor owed me to get that warrant."

The fire drained from her. "If no one else cares about what happened, doesn't that tell you anything?"

"It tells me that they want to move on with their lives and forget the war ever happened." He flexed his long fingers. "But it did happen. Maybe I can't fix a thousand other injustices that happened during that war, but I can fix this one."

Through the bedroom window, the whinny of horses sliced through her jumbled thoughts. Someone was here! She said a prayer of thanks.

He glanced to the door, his jaw working. *Think.* "That's likely a patient."

Not waiting for his response, she hurried to the bedroom door.

Rafferty grabbed her arm, stopping her dead in her tracks. "What's the rush, Mrs. Carter?"

"It could be serious."

His expression was unreadable. "Let's have a look and see."

She nodded and, when he released her, she moved to the front door. It took everything in her not to run. She unbolted the latch, even had it open a crack when Rafferty slammed his palm against the old wood and shoved the door closed.

He hovered so close she could feel his warm breath on her face. "Wait and see. They may just move on."

They can't! She forced herself to face him, to keep the hope out of her voice. His code of honor was his weak spot. "No one comes this late unless they really need my help!"

His gaze darkened as if this unexpected dilemma forced him to make an uncomfortable choice. "You're not the only one who can help."

"If you know so much about me, you know I'm the only one with medical training for a hundred miles," she prodded. "There are several women in town with babies due any day."

He shoved out a ragged sigh, and then pulled her to the window. He drew back the curtain. "Do you recognize them?"

No. "Yes."

Her two visitors carried torches. The riders were roughly dressed like cowhands who'd been on the trail too long. The first man sported a dirty buckskin jacket with fringed edges, Union army pants and a floppy leather hat. His gray horse was so thin it was easy to count each of its ribs.

The second rider was shorter, stouter and wore dusty black pants, a muddy shirt and a long duster. His hat was set low, making it difficult for her to make out his features.

Her heart sank deeper as she stared at the grizzled riders.

"You know men like that?" Rafferty whispered.

"I—I mean, I think I do."

"You get strangers at night often?" Caution crept into his voice.

She moistened her lips. *Rarely.* "It's not uncommon."

He grunted as if he didn't approve. "Find out who it is before you go outside."

"I've never had trouble before."

He guided her to the door. He shifted his range coat back and slid his pistol from its low-riding holster. "A few questions in town and I knew where to find you. Others could have done the same."

She smoothed her hands over her skirts, refusing to let him see that his disclosure had unsettled her. "Why the sudden concern for my safety?"

His grim, unwavering gaze pinned her. "I want you healthy when you stand trial."

Fury knotted her insides. The sooner she got away from him the better.

"Help whoever it is as fast as you can. We're leaving once you're finished."

"Of course," she said quickly.

Rafferty placed his hand on her shoulder as she raised the bar. His fingers tightened enough to hold her attention. "I trusted you once and regretted it. Don't play me for a fool again. Anyone who helps you try to escape will be prosecuted for obstructing justice.''

Rafferty had tracked her one thousand miles and she had no doubt he'd do exactly what he said. He wasn't a man who made idle threats.

As much as she wanted to get away from him, she'd not risk sending a friend to jail. "I understand.''

He stepped back behind the door and slid his gun from his holster. He pushed the hammer back with his thumb.

Drawing in a breath, she opened the door and walked out onto the porch. ''What can I do for you, gentlemen?''

Rafferty's muffled oath gave her a measure of satisfaction. A cold wind rustled her skirts. The first rider nudged his horse forward then stopped. A dozen feet separated them.

''You Meredith Carter?''

''Yes.''

Moonlight flashed on the stranger's gun barrels.

Rafferty reacted instantly. He stormed out to the porch, shoved her aside and knocked her to the porch floor.

And in a second's time, the night exploded with gunfire.

Chapter Three

Meredith dropped to the porch floor and covered her head with her hands. Bullets whirled around her and slammed into the house, spraying splinters of wood. Her belly pressed against the rough-hewn planks until she scooted behind her heavy porch rocker.

"Rafferty!" she shouted. She bit her lower lip, refusing to show fear. "Did you bring these people to my doorstep?"

He fired until his chamber was empty. "No, damn it!"

In the distance, she heard a man yelp in pain. She raised her head enough to see him fall off his horse and land facedown in the dirt. He didn't move again.

"Larry!" the first rider shouted to the dead

man. "Don't tell me you got yourself killed." He fired at Rafferty but the pistol's hammer struck an empty chamber.

Rafferty took advantage and quickly reloaded. He cocked his gun's hammer, jumped to his feet and fired again at the remaining gunman.

The first bullet hit the gunman in the shoulder and the second his chest. A look of shock registered on the outlaw's face before he fell to the ground dead.

Rafferty's stance was rigid. An eerie silence descended over the yard as he kept his gun trained on the gunmen and waited for any signs of life.

Nothing.

Moving with an uneven gait, Rafferty crossed the yard, his gun still drawn. He kicked the first gunman, who stared sightlessly into the night sky.

Again, nothing.

Rafferty shifted his attention to the other stranger, whose leg had gotten twisted under him when he'd fallen off his horse. He pushed him over on his back. A large red bloom darkened the stranger's gray shirt above his heart.

Meredith rose and moved to the edge of the porch. In the moonlight, she could make out Larry's face. Pockmarked and covered with gray stubble, his expression was oddly relaxed now. The sight of death always unsettled her.

Meredith brushed a loose strand of hair from her face. "They're dead?"

"Yes."

Rafferty picked up their guns and tossed them near the house. His body was taut with fury and she suspected he was angry enough to kill them a second time if he could.

She held onto the porch rail for support. "Who were those men?"

"I don't know." With deliberate slowness, he shoved his gun into his holster then picked up one of the still-burning torches. He knelt down and reached in the breast pocket of the man closest to him. Finding nothing, he dug through the other man's pockets until he found a piece of paper. He unfolded the paper and scowled. "But they knew who you were."

She inched down the stairs, careful to keep her distance from Rafferty. He may have saved her, but he was still dangerous. "A lot of people in this valley know me. I told you there's no doctor and people come to me when they are sick or hurt."

Rafferty waved the paper. "How many folks

out here receive telegrams from Washington that have directions to this cabin?''

She bit her lip. "Why would someone from Washington send them to see me?"

As if speaking to a child, he said, "They came here with only one purpose—to kill you."

The idea that she'd come so close to dying made her tremble. "You saved my life."

"I'd say so."

The arrogant tone in his voice galled her. She hated owing him. "Thank you."

His gaze swung from the dead bodies to her. The fury was gone and in its place was coldness that chilled her. "Consider us even."

He referred to that day two years ago in Libby Prison when she'd come to tend Lieutenant Ward. She had saved Ward's life and she'd sensed he despised owing anyone. "Why would anyone want to kill me?"

He tucked the paper into his pocket. "Can't say. But I'll make a point to find out when we get to Washington."

Panic roiled inside her as she tried to keep her voice cool and steady. "We need to call the sheriff."

"The sheriff can sort this mess out for himself."

"But he'll have questions," she said. "And those men need to be buried."

"None of that is my problem now." The torch in hand, he approached her. "We're leaving."

Meredith edged along the porch rail. Her gaze darted to the dark woods and a small path that led to the river. She clung to anything that might delay their departure. "I haven't finished packing."

Light from the torch hardened the planes of his face. "Time's up. We're leaving."

If he got too close, he could easily grab her, and then there'd be no escape. "There are things I'm going to need."

As if reading her mind, he closed the ten-foot gap between them in a flash and grabbed her arm. "Don't try me, angel." He yanked her toward the steps and winced.

Her gaze involuntarily dropped to his hand and discovered that blood stained his fingers and left side. "You've been shot."

He didn't even bother to glance at the blood on his shirtsleeve. "Doesn't change anything," he said through gritted teeth.

He nudged her to the back of the house. Even wounded, he still possessed the strength of a bear.

Behind the house stood a tall, white mare, fully

saddled, her bridle twisted around a branch.
"Time to go, angel."

Panic bloomed afresh in Meredith. She dug her
heels into the dirt. She tried to pry his fingers from
her arm. When they wouldn't budge, she
screamed.

"Yell all you want," Rafferty said. "No one's
here. Unless the men I just killed have friends out
there waiting for us. They might come running."

She stumbled. "They came alone."

He blocked her between the horse and his body.
"Did they?"

"You're just trying to scare me."

He dropped the torch and stamped out its flame.
"I'm trying to keep you alive." He took the
horse's reins. "Now climb up."

Meredith searched for anything that could reach
him. "You'll bleed to death on the trail. You'll
never make it to Washington."

In the moonlight, she could see that sweat glistened on his brow. "I'll make it," he said, steel
in his voice. "Climb up."

Her heart sank as she reached for the pommel.
Her slick palms gripped the leather. "Rafferty,
please listen to me. I hated the Union and what it
did to my life, but I never betrayed you or those
prisoners."

"That's for a court to decide."

His voice had grown ragged. His breathing sounded more labored. Rafferty couldn't hide the fact that he was in pain. Few could sustain blood loss and still keep moving.

"It's a matter of time before you pass out."

He leaned closer. His chest plastered against her back. "I'm touched by your concern."

She tried to reason with him. "Rafferty, you're a strong man. You could carry on for hours, days maybe, before you collapse. Beyond the county's borders, I'm lost. If you faint, I won't know enough to get us back to town."

"I'm not going to pass out."

Spoken like a man. "At least let's spend the night here. I can patch you up."

White teeth glistened in the moonlight. "You're the last person I want cutting into me."

"I can help you."

He snorted. "Into an early grave?"

He was as flexible as granite. "What if there are other men out there waiting for us? You're in no shape to fight. *Our* best hope is to get into town." In truth, it was *her* best hope.

"Nice try." He nodded at the saddle. "Now get up there before I hog-tie you."

Escape, now or never, Meredith thought.

She shoved her full weight into his wounded side. Her palm struck Rafferty's bullet wound dead center. He stumbled back and hit the dirt hard with a grunt. His horse snorted and pawed her feet into the dirt.

"Damn you," he roared.

She bolted for the woods.

But Rafferty's reflexes were too quick. He grabbed the hem of her skirt and yanked. The sound of fabric tearing mingled with her screams. "Let me go!"

"I've come too far to lose you now!"

He yanked her backward, grabbed her ankle and sent her toppling off balance. She fell hard on her hands and knees.

Meredith clawed at the dirt, trying to stand, but his grip was too strong. "You're insane!"

Cringing, he hauled himself to his feet. He planted a booted foot on the hem of her skirt, trapping her. "No. Just determined."

He stood still for a moment, looming over her as he struggled with the pain. The blood smearing his shirt and face made him look more like a monster than a man.

Finally he caught his breath. He pulled her to her feet and toward his horse. Her body was up against the horse's well-muscled haunch. "Please,

Rafferty. You're not seeing reason. I can help you.''

''Like you did two years ago?'' He nodded toward the stirrup. His lips were pale. She heard the clink of iron and glanced down as he drew handcuffs from his saddlebags.

Once he put those on her, she'd never get away. ''If you die on the trail, I'll not only be lost but shackled to your dead body.''

He leaned against her, using his weight to hold her still. ''Touching. Give me your hand.''

''Please, don't do this.'' Meredith fisted her fingers.

''Give me your hand, damn you.'' Pain punctuated his words. Before she could respond, he roughly took her wrist and clamped the ring closed. The cold metal grated the tender underside of her skin.

Time was running out. Once the other wrist was secure, he had her.

As he fumbled for the second cuff, dangling from a one-foot chain, she raised her foot and drove her heel hard into his shin.

The blow sent him reeling back a step. Just enough time for her to skirt along the horse and away from Rafferty.

Meredith turned and started to run, the handcuff

dangling from her wrist. Dread made her clumsy and she tripped over a small stump. She took several extralarge steps before she caught herself and regained control of her footing. Breathing hard, she set her sights on the woods, which ringed the field surrounding her ranch.

Less than one hundred yards away.

There was a stream beyond the woods. More trees. Rocks. In the dark there were a hundred places to hide.

She felt as if she were trapped in a nightmare as the bramble and tree limbs caught her skirt hem. The stand of trees was getting closer. Soon she'd be safe. Panting, she pressed her fingers into the soft flesh under her ribs, trying to soothe the pain in her side brought on by running.

Fifty yards to go. Just hang on.

Rafferty's footsteps thundered behind her and crunched sticks. She dared a glance over her shoulder. He was gaining on her. His breathing was hard and labored, but he was moving fast.

Too fast.

He'd catch her if she didn't hurry.

She dug deep and ran faster.

The unsteady thud of his boots grew louder and her terror nearly choked what breath she had from her lungs. She tried not to think about Rafferty's fierce gaze.

Concentrate on the woods. You'll be safe there. Twenty yards.

He was getting closer. This time, she didn't dare glance back. She could sense him closing in behind her.

Ten yards.

In the woods she could find a stick, a rock, some kind of weapon to defend herself.

Five yards.

Her strength drained from her body. Please, just a few more feet.

Rafferty's fingers scraped her shoulders. "Damn you, stop."

She screamed and skittered out of his grasp. "Leave me alone!"

He grabbed a handful of her hair and she felt a savage jolt. Pain seared through Meredith's head, bringing her to a dead stop.

Rafferty pulled her until her back smacked into his hard chest. She gulped in air as her heart battered her chest.

The buttons of his jacket dug into her flesh as his lips brushed her ear. His masculine scent mingled with his sweat and the tang of blood.

"Enough." He was breathing as hard as she

was. He had to be exhausted. "Put the other cuff on."

Meredith's knees shook. For the space of a dozen heartbeats, she froze. This couldn't be happening.

Her hesitation irritated Rafferty. "Now!"

With a trembling hand, she fished around for the other manacle. "Listen to me, please. I had nothing to do—"

"Quiet."

Her body began to shake. He was like a wounded animal, dangerous and very unpredictable.

He shifted, and she realized her upper right shoulder was wet. She touched her fingertips to the damp fabric and realized she was covered in blood. His blood. "If my hands are shackled, I can't help you."

"We've already been through that. You're not getting anywhere near me with a knife."

In the pale moonlight his face had the pallor of chalk. He wasn't standing as steady as he had been. "You're dying."

His eyes narrowed, and he winced as he straightened his shoulders. "Put the cuff on."

If she stalled a few more minutes, he'd pass

out. She reached for the cuff dangling from the end of a chain. "You can't ride."

He loomed over her. "I'll ride."

The metal bracelet swung from the end of the chain, a perfect weapon. "You can barely stand."

Moonlight sparkled on the metal cuff. "If you hit me with that, I'll make what the Yanks did to Atlanta look like a cakewalk." He grabbed her wrist and the cuff. Snaking it around her wrist, he clicked it into place.

Meredith's heart sank. She was trapped.

Silent, he grabbed the chain dangling between the handcuffs and headed for the cabin. Any other man would have collapsed by now, but Rafferty kept moving, a man possessed.

They had reached his horse, when he stumbled. He tilted his head into the horse's neck, as if trying to draw strength. The mare pawed at the dirt, upset by the smell of blood.

"Rafferty, let me help you," Meredith begged. The iron cuffs chaffed her skin.

"Don't touch me," he rasped. As if to prove he was still in control, he stepped back from the horse and drew his gun. "Climb up."

The chain dangled between her wrists, and her gaze was trained on the gun. As she raised her leg and started to push up, he reholstered the gun, then dropped to his knees.

Meredith hesitated, waiting.

Rafferty rolled on his back, tried to sit up one last time then collapsed, unconscious.

Meredith backed away from the horse and Rafferty. The manacle weighed heavily on her wrists. She needed the key, which was likely in his pocket.

She waited. He didn't look as if he was breathing.

Meredith knelt beside him and pressed trembling fingers to his neck. He was alive.

Unable to bring herself to look at his face, she lifted his coat and dug her fingers into his breast pocket. Her fingers brushed metal and she fished out a key.

"Thank you. Thank you," she whispered. She shoved the key in the lock, twisted and the lock clicked open. "Thank you."

Meredith scrambled to unfasten the second manacle and dropped the handcuffs to the ground. She was so relieved to be free of Rafferty she nearly wept.

She rubbed her wrists, now marred by red bands of irritated flesh, rose and backed away.

Feeling more in control, she calmed.

She watched the shallow rise and fall of Rafferty's chest. Chewing her lip, she lifted the flap of his shirt and inspected the wound, now bleeding badly.

"By all rights I should just leave you." She looked at his face, which appeared paler than before. If she didn't intervene quickly, he'd die. "Why should I save someone who wants to cart me off to jail?"

Even as she uttered the words to the unconscious man, she touched his forehead with her hand. Cold. *Too, too* cold.

She had two choices. One: take Rafferty's horse, ride into town and fetch the sheriff. But the round-trip ride would take at least an hour. And in that time Rafferty would likely bleed to death.

Of course, Rafferty's death would solve all her problems. With him gone, she doubted anyone else would pick up his misguided cause for justice. She'd be free to live her life without the specter of the war looming over her.

Choice number two: stay and try to save his life.

If by some miracle, she managed to patch him up, he would take her back to Washington and force her to stand trial. His bullheaded single-mindedness wouldn't be swayed by her kindness.

The choice seemed simple.

She started to walk away and then stopped. He was dying. Only she could save him now.

Returning to his side, she knelt beside him. "I should leave you," she said, even as she pushed back his jacket and inspected his wound again.

His eyes opened to narrow slits. He was clear, focused. "This is your chance to finish the job."

Ignoring him, she moved behind him and placed her hands under his arms. She tried to lift him, but weakened, he was heavier than lead.

Sweat trickled between her breasts as she caught her breath. It would be impossible to patch him up outside. "You're going to have to help me."

"Why?"

"You have to sit up."

Too weary to protest, he let her coax him to a sitting position. He grunted in agony. He tried to keep his head steady, but pain forced him to rest it against her shoulder. She waited until he'd caught his breath before she wrapped his good arm around her slender shoulder.

He straightened. Clearly, sheer will and vinegar drove him now. "Going to kill me now, angel?"

"And have your ghost haunting me forever? I

don't think so." She tightened her hold on him. "Try to stand."

Her muscles strained as she pulled him up. With her help, he staggered to his feet. The simple task took the wind out of both of them. He leaned heavily on her. Her feet braced apart, her knees threatened to buckle under his weight.

"Don't do me any favors, angel."

"Shut up, Rafferty, and save your strength."

"For what? You said it yourself, I'm dying." He didn't sound afraid, but annoyed.

"You're too heavy for me to carry and I need you to walk inside."

He didn't resist as she wrapped his arm around her shoulders. "Why?"

"Because, like it or not, I'm going to save your stupid life."

Chapter Four

Rafferty leaned heavily on Meredith as they climbed the three front porch steps. His leaden feet caught on the top step and he stumbled, forcing her to draw on every ounce of her strength to steady him. She kicked open the front door with her foot.

Inside, he swayed and blinked as he stared at the room. "The world is spinning."

She knew what he was thinking. "The blood loss is making you dizzy," she said, trying to catch her own breath.

"I'm not dizzy."

So, so stubborn. "You're not going to will this problem away, Rafferty."

He swallowed. "You're enjoying this."

"Every moment," she said tartly.

He just barely made it to her bed. She shoved her hastily packed carpetbag to the floor, just as he collapsed against the squeaky springs and dropped his head back against the pillow. He expelled a ragged breath. They were both soaked in his blood.

She laid her warm fingers on his forehead. It was cold, clammy, and his hands trembled. "Hang on, Rafferty."

A shiver shuddered through his body. "I'm so damn cold," he said, his teeth chattering.

Meredith lit every lantern she could find in the cabin and stoked the fire in her cookstove. After she set a filled kettle on the oven top, she laid another clean kitchen knife on the hot burner. As the blade and water heated, she collected her salves, threads and a sharp needle and carried them to the bedroom. She set them all on the small table next to Rafferty's bed.

Rafferty had passed out. His cheeks were sunken and the circles under his eyes were black. He was as still as death. She touched his chest to make sure he was still alive. He was alive. Barely.

His eyes opened and he tried to sit up. "Where the hell am I?"

Meredith pushed him back against the sheets.

Even in his weakened state he was a strong as a bull. "You're safe."

"My shoulder is on fire."

Touch often had the power to calm a restless patient. She laid her warm palm on his forehead. "I'm going to make that better."

He started to struggle. "Not you. Never you."

She didn't argue but cupped his face in her hands, forcing his gaze to meet hers. "Rafferty, the more you move, the more you bleed. You must trust me."

Something she couldn't define flickered in his cold blue eyes. "I made that mistake once."

"You don't have a choice this time."

"Like hell. I'm leaving."

Men were her worst patients. She changed tactics as the teakettle started to whistle. "Fine, go ahead and leave."

She went to the kitchen and pulled the bubbling kettle off the burner then returned to the bedroom. She found Rafferty trying to sit up.

Folding her arms over her chest, she waited. If he managed to stand, it would be a miracle.

He made it up on his elbows, then winced and fell back against the pillows. In a weak gesture, he smacked the sheets with his fist.

Satisfied that she'd proved her point and that

he wasn't going anywhere, she reached for his boot and tugged it off. "If I wanted you dead, Captain Rafferty, I'd have put a bullet in you *outside*. Think about it. Why go through the trouble to drag you into my house and *then* kill you? I'd only have to haul your dead body *back* outside." With a grunt she pulled off his second boot. "I've already got to dig two graves for those two men you killed. And I'd rather not have to dig one for you."

He relaxed against the pillow as if he saw the logic in her words. "This doesn't change anything. I'm still taking you to Washington."

"You're welcome." Meredith reached for his gun belt.

He grabbed her hand. "Not my guns."

"I'll hang them on the headboard. You can reach them at any time."

He nodded, too weak to talk. He released her and let his hand drop.

Once she'd hung the gun belts on the bedpost, she took the scissors from her uncle's doctor's bag. Carefully she slid the blade under the rough fabric of his shirt and started to cut. The muscles in Rafferty's flat belly tensed as she sliced through the center of his shirt.

Removing the shirt remnants, she tossed the

soiled clothes into a soggy heap on the floor. Buttery lantern light glowed on his muscled chest covered with a thick mat of hair. An old scar slashed across his right side, likely the mark of a bayonet, and on his left arm a small cluster of small scars—buckshot.

So much pain.

Meredith's stomach roiled as she wiped the blood from the bullet wound. The bullet had gone clean through, but the wound bled badly. She knew she'd have to cauterize the wound and dreaded it. She had helped her uncle treat hundreds of bullet wounds during the war, but she'd never developed the strong stomach her uncle had had for this kind of work.

Rafferty moistened his dry lips. "What are you going to do?"

With the back of her hand, she pushed the stray wisps of hair off her face. "I've got to stop the bleeding."

"Good. Then we'll leave."

Meredith nearly laughed. His mind was so befuddled he had no idea how desperate his situation was.

As a precaution, she tied his hands to the metal frame of the bed. She checked and rechecked her knots then moved to the stove to inspect the blade. Searing heat rose from the red-hot blade.

It was ready.

She wrapped a tea cloth around the handle and returned to Rafferty. "Captain, I'm going to cauterize the wound now."

He opened his eyes, the distant hazy look telling her he didn't understand.

She straddled Rafferty's large muscled frame, sacrificing propriety for practicality. She was a small woman and often had to use all her weight to handle patients who sometimes were too sick or too delirious to accept help.

She squeezed her legs around his waist, knowing he'd buck like a bull in seconds. "I'm sorry."

She laid the hot blade on the wound.

Rafferty's eyes flew open and he arched his head back into the pillow. The veins in his neck bulged and his hands strained against their bindings, but he didn't scream out.

Meredith struggled to keep her balance as she pressed the blade deeper into the wound. The smell of burnt flesh assailed her nostrils and she had to fight her own nausea. She counted to five slowly, just as her uncle had taught her, then pulled the blade away.

Rafferty's body, now soaked with sweat, went limp. Mercifully, he'd passed out.

Meredith released the breath she'd been holding and slid off him down to the floor. Her limbs felt weak and her own body drained, as if she'd pressed the blade to her own flesh.

Setting the knife aside, she inspected the wound. The bleeding had stopped, though the skin was seared and badly burned. Thankfully, she'd not have to repeat the cauterization.

It took her another half hour to clean and stitch Rafferty's wound. She inspected her neat row of stitches alongside the blade's angry burn. Another scar would mar his flesh, but hopefully he'd survive and regain full use of his arm.

Too weary to stand any longer, she sat on the edge of the bed. She spread a soothing salve over his shoulder. His body was cool to the touch now, but later the fever would come. The fight to save Rafferty was far from over.

She replaced the salve on the nightstand. Even unconscious, his brow was furrowed and his lips turned down. She brushed her hand over his cheek. "Looks like we're stuck with each other for the next few days, Captain."

And if he survived the fever and recovered?

Then what?

And if he died?

Could she live with herself?

By the time she'd done all she could for Rafferty, the sun had risen. Meredith wanted nothing more than to sleep, but knew she couldn't leave the dead gunmen lying in her front yard. Soon the sun would be high and hot in the sky. She turned her sights to the gruesome task of burying them.

As she moved across the front yard, she saw Rafferty's white mare. She stood near a stand of grass chewing on a stand of tall grass.

The horse lifted its head to stare at Meredith. It snorted.

"I'll deal with you later," Meredith said.

At the sound of her voice, Shorty, like an old man with creaky bones, meandered out of the barn. He thumped his tail in greeting.

Meredith patted the dog, then with Blue's help, she dragged the men's bodies to the field close to the river, where the soil tended to be soft. She dug a hole and buried them as best she could, even taking a moment to say a word or two over their graves.

When she, Shorty and Blue returned to the yard, it was near noon and Rafferty's white horse was waiting for them. She swished as if she were annoyed or late for an appointment. She turned Blue loose in the corral and took her first good look at the mare. The animal's coat glistened. "Well, aren't you a beauty."

Taking the horse's reins, she tugged, but unlike Blue, the horse didn't budge at first. It took another firm jerk of the reins to get her moving toward the corral. The horse sauntered through the gate as though she was a queen. She pawed at the dirt and snorted as Meredith unsaddled her.

Meredith hung Rafferty's saddle and bags on the corral fence. From the barn, she retrieved hay and a few apples for the horses and jerky for the dog.

After she stuffed hay into the feed bins, she knelt by Shorty. "Been a day hasn't it, old man? Been a long time since we had so much company."

The old dog barked. She gave him extra jerky and he took it. His head lowered, he hurried to the barn to eat the treat.

Meredith smiled. "I thought you'd like that."

Behind her, she heard the rustle of leaves and the snap of twigs. She rose. Something was out there, moving around.

Fearing more gunmen had arrived, she turned and scanned the field and woods trying to spot any unexpected guests. Rafferty would be no help.

She hurried inside and retrieved an old shotgun that had belonged to her uncle. She'd not cleaned the gun since her uncle's death and wondered if it could still shoot. She raised it, hoping it was enough to scare off any intruder.

"Who's there?" she shouted.

To her surprise, a rickety nag limped out of the woods. She recognized the animal. It had belonged to one of the men Rafferty had killed. Its ribs poked against its sagging skin. Its coat was dull and its hooves unshod.

Meredith sighed. Torn between crying and laughing her relief, she leaned the gun against the porch rail and crossed the yard to the animal. "Who do we have here?" She skimmed her hand over the horse's haunch. "You're going to need a good brushing and a bath."

Unresponsive, the horse stared at the ground.

Meredith inspected a gash cut into the horse's side with a whip. That would need medicine or it would become infected. Mentally she calculated the time it would take to care for the animal.

She took the horse by the reins. "I don't need the extra work of another horse," she said as she guided the horse to the corral and unsaddled it.

Hands on hips, she studied the pitiful creature. "Mrs. Harper was right," she muttered as she poured a bucket of fresh water into the horse trough. "I am a sucker for a lost cause."

Rafferty's mare nickered as if she took exception to the new guest.

"Don't complain to me," Meredith said. "I'm not too crazy about having you here, either."

Rafferty's mare snorted.

Blue whinnied.

"Yeah, yeah. Get in line." She unsaddled the nag and draped the saddle and bags on the fence next to Rafferty's.

Despite her complaints and her fatigue, the scents of hay, horse and leather eased her frayed nerves a notch. Around the animals, she felt like her old self—everything was calm.

Blue pawed at the ground and snorted. Laughing, Meredith pulled an apple from her apron pocket and held it out for the animal.

"Looks like we've got more company, Blue." The gelding gobbled the apple, happily nuzzling Meredith's hand with his warm, wet lips.

Rafferty's horse whinnied. Meredith pulled out an apple for the white mare. The proud, tall animal didn't approach as Blue had.

Palm flat, Meredith waited patiently for the horse to get used to her. "It's for you."

The animal stared at her, breathing hard.

"Oh for pity's sake," Meredith said, losing patience. "It's just an apple, not poison. I don't need trouble from you."

The horse sniffed the apple.

"Just as distrustful as your wounded Yank master."

Coaxed by the soft sound of Meredith's voice, the animal licked the apple, then looked at her with clear, brown eyes as if trying to judge whether or not she was being tricked. Finally the mare accepted the treat.

"See? No poison. When are you and Rafferty going to learn I'm no threat to anyone?"

As Meredith raised her hand to scratch the horse between the ears, the animal tensed but didn't back away. Going slowly, she gently stroked the rich coat.

Turning from the mare, she focused on the gunman's horse. Though the horse wasn't more than five or six years old, it was clearly lame. It wouldn't be good for any farm work and Meredith was surprised it had been able to carry a rider.

Meredith dug out her largest apple slice for the

underfed horse. Sadness tugged at her as the animal gobbled up the treat.

She looked at its cracked hooves. "New shoes might help those feet of yours."

The nag nudged Meredith's hand, savoring every bit of attention. "I can't keep calling you horse, or nag. You're going to need a name." Laughing, she gave the horse an extra apple. "How about Sam?"

Sam's velvet nose nuzzled her hand, then chomped on his apple.

"When I get to town I'll see if the blacksmith can make you a new pair of shoes. I stitched his hand a few months back and he said to call if I needed anything."

Moving to leave, she spotted Rafferty's saddlebags alongside the gunman's. She traced her fingers over the two sets. She'd have to go through the gunman's bag eventually to find out who they were, but curiosity had her reaching for Rafferty's bag first.

Rafferty's horse snorted her disapproval.

Guiltily she looked over her shoulder at the mare. "I'm not taking anything. I'm just having a peek. No harm done. You don't tell and I won't tell."

She slid her hand into the worn leather pouch

and pulled out a tobacco bag, a large wedge of jerky wrapped in canvas, a pencil, notebook, extra bullets and a large knife tucked in an ornate silver sheath.

She inspected the knife case, marveling at the workmanship. Rafferty didn't strike her as the kind of man who'd own something so ornate or fussy, but then she reminded herself she really didn't know anything about him. She drew the blade out and inspected the razor-edge tip, which glittered dangerously in the fading sunlight. She pressed the tip to her thumb and flinched when it pricked her skin. A drop of blood dripped from the tiny cut. Lovely, but very deadly.

Meredith carefully shoved the sharp knife back into its sheath then put both in her apron pocket. She sucked the blood from the tip of her thumb as she turned her attention to Rafferty's book. A quick glance told her it was a journal.

Rafferty's mare whinnied.

"I know. It wouldn't be right to look at it," she muttered. She thumbed through the pages. Without reading the private words, she noted the bold, deep imprint of his handwriting. A piece of paper fluttered to the ground.

Kneeling, she picked it up. It was a list of men's names.

Ballintine, John, 2/15/63, New York, 1st Regiment, Age 24

Each name included the same information—the man's rank, a date, a regiment and his age.

Why did Rafferty carry the list with him? Had the men served under him? Been friends?

And then it struck her. She knew. These were the names of men who had been killed during the prison escape.

This list was his way of remembering the dead.

She closed the book and tucked it back in the bag.

Rafferty's blood felt as if it were on fire. His mouth was as dry as cotton and his tongue swollen.

He'd lost his bearings. And time had stopped for him. He wasn't sure if he were alive, in heaven or in hell.

Hell.

He almost laughed at the thought.

Four long years of war had been hell on earth and it would just be his luck to end up in the fiery underworld.

"Water." His voice was little more than a hoarse whisper and he barely recognized it.

Maybe he was dead. And if he were in hell, the chances of getting water were slim.

He was surprised to feel soft fingers cup the back of his head and lift it. A metal cup pressed against his parched lips and cool water trickled drop by drop into his mouth. Greedy, he lifted his head, hungry for more.

"Go slow." The woman's voice was as sweet as an angel's.

Angel.

She gently laid his head against the pillow. Her feather-light fingers brushed the hair off his forehead.

He'd have opened his eyes if his lids weren't so damn heavy. Even his arms felt as if they'd been forged by iron.

"Am I dead?"

She laughed softly. She touched his brow. "No, just very sick."

"Am I going to die?"

She hesitated. "I don't know."

He didn't like the honesty, but appreciated it.

He was so damn tired.

So weary of the fight.

Of being alone.

Angel.

He remembered exactly where he was.

He couldn't stop fighting. He had to take her to Washington. To see this nightmare through.

Unable to think anymore, he drifted and let the blackness overtake him.

Chapter Five

By sunset, Rafferty's fever raged.

Meredith was dozing in a rocker beside his bed when he began shouting in his sleep. "Sergeant, get the men behind the ridge! We'll lose every one if we don't take cover."

She jerked forward. Stiff from her nap in the rocker, she winced as she leaned forward. After working the kinks from her shoulder, she laid her hand on his forehead. His skin was hot, damp with sweat.

"It's all right, Captain," she said. "I'll get you more water."

His head rocked from side to side, his face contorted. "It's not safe! Get them behind the ridge, Sergeant."

He was delirious. "Captain, it is okay."

She poured water into a cup and, lifting his head, touched it to his lips.

He refused to drink and then his eyes opened. Their blue depths looked clouded with fever. "Get that away from me."

"You have to drink."

"Get moving, now!"

At the sharp order, she straightened and set the cup on the nightstand. There was no arguing with him now. The fever had a hold on him. Better keep him calm. "The men are safe, Captain. They're behind the ridge."

The tense muscles in his body eased. He swallowed. "Thank God."

She filled the porcelain washbasin with cool water and set it by his bed. Dipping a clean rag in the water, she rung it out and started to wipe his hot skin.

She repeated the washing a dozen times throughout the night. He slipped into a restless slumber, starting at every sound. Often he cried out for his men, always worried about their safety.

There wasn't much she could do but sit, watch and hope he was strong enough to fight the infection. James, her late husband, like so many strong men she'd nursed, had survived the initial injury but later died from the fever.

She brushed a lock of damp hair off Rafferty's face. "Don't die on me now, Rafferty. Join me and we'll fight this fever together."

Even through the fever, Rafferty seemed to respond to her. He turned his face so his cheek brushed the back of her hand and mumbled something unintelligible.

A smile touched her lips. "Somehow, we'll make it through this."

He relaxed back into the pillows, slipping into a deep sleep.

In the stillness of the evening, she sat next to his bed. Until now, she'd been so busy trying to save his life that she'd not taken the time to study his features. Now, she couldn't tear her gaze from him.

His face had filled out since his time in Libby Prison, but it remained all hard angles. His nose was slightly crooked, as if it had been broken in a brawl, and there was a thick ragged scar over his left eye. His hair was as black as coal and his lips full and soft, now that he wasn't frowning.

She'd heard the prison guards talking about Rafferty. Many of his captors feared him and were careful always to have extra guards on hand when rations for his cell block were delivered.

James was so unlike Rafferty.

Her late husband had been a statesman, a politician at heart, and he had taken up arms reluctantly. His features had been softer, more refined and his eyes had been an enviable green, his smile quick. He had been graced with a charm that drew people naturally to him.

James was the poet.

Rafferty was the warrior.

She turned Rafferty's hand over. It was rough, callused, like a brawler's. James's hands had been as soft as butter.

"Angel," he whispered, as if he sensed she'd been thinking about him.

Meredith started. She dropped his hand against the mattress. She felt as though she'd been caught with her hand in the cookie jar.

It was wrong to compare Rafferty and James.

James had cherished her, understood her and she'd vowed to love him forever.

Rafferty hated her. He was bent on destroying her life. And soon she'd be forced to leave him.

Rafferty dreamed of Meredith, as he had so many nights these past two years. Every detail of her face was as clear as if she were with him. Golden flecks in her green eyes, silken auburn curls, and skin as soft as rose petals teased his senses.

His body hardened.

In his dreams, Meredith came to him wearing a transparent chemise that cupped her rosy breasts and skimmed over her delicate hips. Her hair flowed loose, dangling beyond her shoulders.

Each night was the same.

He'd roll her on her back as she willingly wrapped her arms around his neck, drawing him close, molding her body to his. He savored her scent, a soft blend of lilacs and woman. As he pushed her legs open with his thigh, she'd tease him with a passionate kiss, caressing the inside of his mouth with her tongue, nipping his skin with her even, white teeth.

He suckled her breast. She arched. Cried out his name. His erection throbbed until he thought he'd go mad, and then he'd drive into her. Her tight body, wrapped around him, welcomed his invasion.

Her passion matched his and together they rode the wave of desire until their climaxes overtook them both.

He damned himself for his weakness, but he always anticipated her visits and never denied her.

She'd bewitched him.

She was a Siren, destined to lure him to his destruction.

And he didn't care.

Rafferty woke with a start just after dawn. He didn't need to raise his head to know that his mind had cleared. The fever that had possessed him had passed.

Immediately, he was aware of two things.

Meredith was nearby.

And his hands were tied.

He jerked at his bindings and tried to twist his hand free but the knots held. He yanked again and again, but only managed to exhaust what little strength he'd gained and stir the pain in his shoulder.

He fell back against the pillows. "Meredith!" he shouted.

Soft footsteps clicked across the wood floor and then Meredith appeared. She leaned against the door frame, drying her hands with a checkered cloth. "You're awake."

Her hair, a thick coppery mass, was pinned on top of her head. The style framed her pale face and defined her high cheekbones and bright eyes. She'd bathed and changed into a blue calico dress that hugged her waist and the swell of her breasts.

Rafferty grew hard looking at her.

He flexed his fingers. Dreams were one thing, reality another.

The sooner he got her to Washington and out of his life, the better. "Untie me!"

She lingered in the doorway, seemingly unsure the ropes would hold. "You're in a foul mood."

"I'm in a damned fine mood."

She lifted an eyebrow. "You are not."

Rafferty worked his jaw, forcing his clenched fingers to relax. He counted to ten. "Why did you tie my hands?"

"When you were sick, you were delirious. I didn't want you to tear your stitches."

The ropes cut into his wrists as he strained against them. "I'm awake now. *Please* take the *damned* ropes off."

She chewed her bottom lip in indecision then moved closer to the bed. Nimbly she untied the bindings and then stepped back out of his reach.

He rubbed his wrists. Good, now he could get the hell out of here. "We've a stage to make Wednesday in Austin."

A faint smile touched her lips. "It's Thursday. You've been sleeping for four days."

"Four days!" Mentally he assessed the situation. They'd missed their stage in Austin. He'd have to telegram Washington and advise the brass he'd be late.

She twisted the ropes in her hands. "You're lucky to be alive. You do remember that you were shot."

He felt as if a buffalo were standing on his chest, but the memory of the attack was coming back to him. "The gunmen."

"You killed them both. I buried them."

His mind raced faster. "There could be other gunmen."

"No one has come."

He needed to sit up. Pain or no, they had to get moving. "Where is my gun?"

She nodded to the bedpost. "Hanging behind you, just where I left them."

He glanced over his shoulder, saw the gun belt but, for the life of him, couldn't summon the strength to reach them.

"Are you hungry?" Meredith said.

Yes. "No, I want my gun."

She ignored him. "Let me get you a bowl of beef broth."

His stomach growled. "I'm not hungry."

"Of course, you are." She returned to the kitchen. Through the doorway, he watched her dip a ladle into a big cauldron on the stove and spoon a large helping into an oversize tin cup. "You must be starving."

The broth made his mouth water. "I'm fine."

She breezed back into the bedroom. "Food will help your disposition. My uncle was always a bit cranky when he was hungry." She draped a tea towel over her shoulder and picked up a spoon.

He glowered at her. "You're not feeding me."

She stirred the broth. "You have to eat."

Through gritted teeth, he said, "I'll starve before you treat me like an invalid."

Emotion flashed in her eyes. "I'm only trying to help."

"I don't want your help." He felt as helpless as he had in Libby Prison.

She set the cup down so hard on the nightstand that hot soup sloshed over the side. "Fine, Captain. Feed yourself. Walk around the cabin. Strap on your guns and go find a bad guy."

"I will!" Rafferty reached for the edge of the blanket and realized for the first time that he was completely naked. "If you think modesty is going to stop me, you're wrong."

"Go ahead," she said, shrugging. "It's nothing I haven't seen before."

Rafferty started to sit up and lifted the covers. Immediately he stopped. His stomach flip-flopped. The earth shifted violently under his feet. He closed his eyes and swallowed.

"Room spinning now?" she said too sweetly.

He fell back against the pillows. "What the hell have you done to me?"

She planted her hand on her hip. "The gunmen did the damage, not me."

He sucked in a deep breath and, wincing, tried to push himself up again. This time he stayed up for nearly thirty seconds before he started to sway badly. He'd have toppled out of bed if Meredith hadn't grabbed a hold of him and steadied him. Unable to help himself, he leaned into her for support. "I hate this."

Gently she eased him back down onto the pillow. "Let me get you an extra pillow or two." Her voice had lost the edge of irritation. "Sitting up is about as much as you're going to be able to handle today."

She retrieved two down pillows from the chest at the edge of the bed. Gently she raised his head and propped the pillows under him.

The support felt good. "How long am I going to be like this?"

"A week, maybe two."

"You're joking."

"Sorry. Your body suffered a great trauma.

The fever you endured would have killed many. You're lucky to be alive.''

''I make my own luck.''

She handed him the napkin. ''Not this time.'' Smiling sweetly, she picked up the soup cup. ''You can feed yourself but chances are, you're not going to be able to hold the cup. Then you're going to spill hot broth all over those nice clean sheets that I put on your bed last night.''

Absently he smoothed his hand over the sheet as if to confirm her statement. They felt soft, smelled fresh, like the outdoors. ''I really hate this.''

''It's not exactly my idea of a good time, either.'' She sat down. ''You have two choices, Rafferty. Starve and stay weak. Eat and get strong.''

After his stay in the prison camp, he'd sworn that he'd never be at anyone else's mercy again. Yet here he was. He cursed the lack of control. ''I'll eat.''

Biting back a grin, she dipped the wide-mouth spoon into the clear broth. Cupping her hand under the spoon, she held it in front of his lips.

He hesitated. ''You're not going to try to poison me are you?''

''Tempting, but no.''

He glared at her, and then accepted the first spoonful. Delicious. "That's not bad."

"Thanks." She ladled another spoon.

He accepted the next mouthful. She scooted a little closer to the bed. He finished the first cup and a second before he felt satisfied.

"More?" she asked.

"No." Food in his belly left him relaxed.

"You've the appetite of a horse."

He lay back. "So they say."

"If you get hungry again, just let me know. There's plenty."

"Thanks."

"You should sleep now."

His body demanded rest, but his mind refused. "You have no idea who those men were that attacked us?"

She shook her head and frowned. "None. I've spent the past four days trying to remember anything that might identify them."

He studied her, searching for signs of deceit. "They knew an awful lot about you."

"I had never seen them before. Why would they want to kill me?"

He cocked an eyebrow. "Maybe I'm not the only enemy from your past."

She sighed, as if she'd considered the idea already. "I know people in Richmond resented my uncle and me for helping the prisoners. Lord knows James could never understand our choices."

He grunted, surprised by his own anger and resentment to her late husband. "I'll bet it was a real thorn in James's side."

She frowned as if she were swept up in memories. Instead of answering him, she shifted the conversation. "I've thought a lot about our predicament these past few days."

He snorted. *"Our predicament?"*

She ignored the sarcasm. "I realize I could plead my innocence until the end of time and it wouldn't sway you. You need facts."

Silent, he stared at her. What game was she playing?

She rubbed her hands down her thighs. "You're good at uncovering facts."

"Damn good. Where's this going?"

"You're just the man I need."

He tensed. "What the hell does that mean?"

She lifted her chin. "I want to hire you."

This was so absurd. "To do what?"

"Prove my innocence."

Chapter Six

"Prove your innocence?" Travis's laughter echoed in the small cabin.

"Yes." She sounded as prickly as an old maid schoolteacher. "I want you to find the real traitor."

His fingers curled into fists. "What kind of trick is this?"

"None," she said, sounding genuinely shocked. "I want to hire you to find the man who really betrayed your men. I do have money."

The woman had nerve. As if he'd ever take her money. "I found what I came looking for."

She leaned forward. "You're wrong about me, Captain Rafferty. I never told the guards about the prison break."

He growled his frustration. "You were married

to a Reb. You made it very clear when you visited the prison that you didn't want to be there."

"All true." She smoothed her hands over her skirt. "I'm guilty of ignoring the suffering of those men for so long. I should have been there to help from the start, like my uncle." She swallowed. "Anger kept me away. But I am not guilty of betraying you. Someone is lying to you. They want you to believe I am guilty."

The softness in her eyes pricked at his heart. He almost believed her. "You *are* guilty."

"I'm not!" She rose and started to leave the room. Her hand on the doorway, she stopped, struggling to regain her composure. "I understand you better than you think."

He flinched. "You know nothing about me."

"The war brought thousands of injustices, most of which will never be righted."

"I don't want to fix everything, just this." His voice was raw, full of unwanted emotion.

"Sending me to prison won't right any wrong. I'm innocent."

"So you keep saying. But you haven't given me one bit of information that proves anything."

"That's why I need you. I need you to help me find the real traitor."

"Lady, I'm too old and too smart to head out on a wild-goose chase."

She sucked in a breath. "Four days you've been here, Rafferty. I could have killed you at any time. For that matter, I could have left you outside to bleed to death."

His gaze pierced her. "Why didn't you?"

She rubbed the back of her neck with her hand. She looked so fragile and tired.

"You are a man of honor," she said softly. "You are trying to correct a wrong."

"Damn right," he growled.

She edged closer to the bed. "I'm not asking you to be my friend or to like me. But for both our sakes we need to find out who the traitor is." She paused. "If you're not willing to do it for me, do it for your men. The dead will know no peace if I go to jail."

Fury choked his heart. "Don't talk about my men. You know nothing about them."

"Yes, I do. They were fathers, brothers, sons and husbands. They were like my James. And they didn't deserve to die so young. They were cheated."

Rafferty's blue eyes blazed with fury. Meredith held her ground, refusing to give quarter. "I'm not trying to make you angry."

A shadow crossed his face. "Lady, you've a knack for it."

There was no reaching him now, no reasoning. Better to retreat, let him cool off, think. She'd approach him later. With a small, polite smile on her lips, she said, "I've got work to do."

Rafferty took a breath. "Don't give me that look."

"What look?"

"Lady of the manor staring at the poor humble stable hand."

"I wasn't—"

"You're thinking I'll cool off and you can circle back later."

She teetered between shock and laughter. "You caught me."

The anger evaporated from his gaze, giving her a measure of hope.

"So, you will help me?"

Instead of answering, he said, "You ever hear of the story of the scorpion and the turtle?"

"No."

"The scorpion and the turtle were each standing on the side of a riverbank. Both had to get to the other side. The scorpion needed the turtle's help because he knew if he tried to cross on his own he'd die. So he convinced the turtle to take him across. He swore to the turtle he wouldn't sting him. So the turtle agreed. Halfway across, the scorpion stung the turtle. As the poison started to spread through the turtle's body, he knew he was going to die. He asked the scorpion why he'd do something so foolish. They both knew when the turtle died the scorpion would drown. The scorpion just shrugged and said he couldn't fight his nature.''

Meredith hadn't missed the hidden meaning. ''Are you the scorpion or am I?''

''Do you really trust me, angel? I could turn on you just like the scorpion.''

''I've no choice.''

''I suppose, right now, neither one of us does.''

''So you're willing to work with me?''

Rafferty studied her outstretched hand then shook his head. ''No.''

When Rafferty awoke the next morning, bright sun splashed over the cabin, brightening the interior. Through his open door, he saw delicate blue flowers in a vase, a red braided rug and yellow-checkered curtains that flapped over the window above the kitchen sink.

Until now, the room had been awash in grays and blacks and had seemed dark and dingy. He was surprised at the colors—how cheery the place was.

His body didn't feel clogged and broken today. A little stiff, but otherwise clear and strong. His head on the pillow, he stretched out his good arm. His muscles protested just a little before the blood flowed through them and eased the tension. His wound felt tight and puckered, but it had lost the heat of yesterday. It didn't take a look under the clean bandage to know it was healing nicely.

He allowed a satisfied grin. Meredith had been wrong when she'd said it would take two weeks for him to mend. The way he felt now, he'd be sitting astride a horse tomorrow. He ran his tongue over his teeth and rubbed his jaw covered in thick stubble. Once he bathed, he'd be just fine.

Without a second thought, Rafferty pushed himself into a sitting position and swung his legs over the side of the bed.

He regretted the move instantly.

His shoulder burned like fire and his legs ached. Lord, he couldn't decide if he felt worse now or when he'd completed an uphill fifty-mile march. He gripped the side of the bed.

He felt worse now. Definitely now.

He'd always been in command of his body. Even in Libby Prison, when he'd been slowed by starvation, he'd forced himself to keep moving. Never had he experienced such a complete sense of helplessness.

Cursing his attacker's bullet, Meredith, the chirping birds outside and his own weakness, he held his ground. He'd never surrendered before and he'd sure as hell not start now.

If the floor would just stop spinning, he'd be fine.

His head bowed, he heard the creak of floor-boards and instantly knew Meredith was close, but he couldn't summon the extra energy to growl at her. He was too busy riding the damn floor, which wouldn't stop bucking.

"You shouldn't be sitting up," she said.

Rafferty sucked in a breath. "I like sitting up."

Fearing the spinning would get worse if he lifted his head, he kept his gaze trained on the floor. He saw the swish of calico move from his doorway into the room.

She set some kind of tray on the nightstand, then placed a cool hand on his forehead. Her skin was a little rough, callused by hard work.

"How's the arm feel?" she asked.

His head was clearing—the damn spinning had slowed a fraction. "Great. Never better." He'd be damned before he'd show her any weakness.

"Really? I'd have guessed you feel like a mule train had hit you today."

Exactly right. "Nope. I feel good." To prove his statement, he lifted his head so that he could see her. He was certain the back of his head fell off, then his left arm.

When he realized he was still intact, the first thing he noticed was her.

So bright, so lovely.

Today she wore her hair down and tied at the nape of her neck with a yellow scarf. The yellow in her dress added color to her cheeks and pinkness to her lips that made him want to touch them.

He'd always had an image of Meredith as physically perfect—small-boned, delicate, smooth hands. She was the kind of woman a man could stare at for a lifetime and never get tired of the view.

Again he grew hard just thinking about her. Grateful for the sheet twisted around his midsection, he clutched it.

She lifted an eyebrow. "You look pale."

"Just need to get into the sun." He spoke with as much force as he could muster.

"So you think you can stand up?"

The disbelief in her voice goaded him into saying something really stupid. "Sure."

"I see."

Damn her, she was enjoying this. Since his refusal to help her, she'd barely spoken five words to him in the past twelve hours.

"My clothes."

"Over there," she said, inclining her head. "All cleaned and mended."

His gaze darted to his clothes, neatly stacked on the cedar chest at the edge of his bed. There was no way in hell he'd ever wrestle his legs into a pair of pants. It was physically impossible.

But he sure wasn't going to back down now. Not again, not in front of her. "If you leave, I'll dress."

She hesitated. "Don't move an inch." Without waiting for a response, she left and returned seconds later with a robe. "Here, put this on."

He considered insisting on his pants but knew, even if she gave them to him, he'd never get them on. It was time to fall back.

Begrudgingly he nodded and allowed her to slip the robe first over his good arm and then, very gingerly, his bad arm.

If Meredith hadn't been so gentle he was certain he'd have passed out from the pain. But she was patient, letting him ease the arm into the soft fabric at his own pace. Sweat covered his brow by the time he'd pulled the robe's folds closed and allowed Meredith to knot its rope belt.

He frowned at the tight knot. "I haven't changed my mind. I won't help you."

She straightened the robe's lapels. "I haven't given up on you yet."

"When I say no, Meredith, I mean no."

She smiled. "Okay."

He didn't know what to make of Meredith. And he was too tired to try and figure the woman out right now. "I want to go outside."

"You're in no condition to go outside," she said matter-of-factly.

She might as well have shouted from the rooftops that he was an invalid.

"Fresh air is just what I need." To prove to himself and to her that he was fine, he started to rise. Fire snapped through his veins, and if she hadn't been standing there waiting he'd have sunk back into the mattress and called it a day. But she was there waiting, doubting, expecting him to fail. So he gritted his teeth and pushed through the pain.

Sweet Lord, for a moment he thought he'd black out, and he swayed.

She was with him in an instant, hugging her side to his, wrapping her arm around his waist.

On reflex, he leaned against her and draped his arm around her narrow shoulder. She wasn't any bigger than a sprite—her head barely reached the top of his shoulders—but her stance was steady and she was strong. And she smelled good. Roses and woman.

Her body nestled against his side, he felt the swell of her breasts pushing against him. They fit well together, as if they'd been made for each other.

Irritated, he stood a little straighter and eased most, not all, of his weight off her. He clamped the folds of his robe closed with his fist.

"Can you walk?" The humor had faded from her voice, replaced by concern.

"Yes." Pure bravado was driving him now and he wasn't sure if his legs would actually work. The door was only fifteen feet way, an impossible journey.

With her help he took a tentative step forward. He paused, making sure he was on steady ground then took another step.

When they reached the door, she stopped. "You've done more than I ever expected today. Best you get back in bed."

He glared down at her and, to his amazement,

was struck by the color of her eyes. Green didn't do them justice. They were more like emeralds.

He dragged his gaze away. "Outside."

She sighed. "You're bullheaded, Captain Rafferty."

"So I've been told." He started to walk. The tightness in his body had eased a fraction.

By some miracle they reached the porch. Rafferty wasn't sure how long it took, minutes likely, but he wouldn't have bet against five or six hours.

The morning sun shone on his face and, eyes closed, he tilted his head back and drank in the warmth. A light breeze brushed his skin. He was feeling better. More in control.

"Let me help you to the rocker," Meredith said.

Rafferty shook his head. "I'd rather stand."

She groaned. "Suit yourself."

Without warning, she moved away, robbing him of her warmth and her support. He staggered, amazed at how much he'd been relying on her.

He sucked in a breath and willed his body to steady, but his muscles would have none of it. He started to sway and realized with horror that he could actually fall.

Meredith placed a chair behind him just as his legs started to crumple. His backside landed in the chair with a thump. He winced and muttered a curse. "I need my gun belt."

"You're welcome," Meredith said.

"Gun."

Muttering, she disappeared into the house and returned moments later with his gun. The gun belt looked ridiculously large on her and she struggled with its awkward weight. He accepted the weapon from her and draped it over his lap. "Thank you."

As she reached for a straw hat hanging on a peg by the front door, he removed the gun from its holster and snapped open the chamber. "It isn't loaded."

She scooped up a basket. "I don't like loaded guns in my house."

He struggled to keep the anger out of his voice. "Two men tried to kill you less than a week ago and you don't keep a loaded gun around?"

"They scare me."

He waited a full minute for her to explain her half-baked reasoning. When she didn't offer any other explanation, he started to load the gun. "Better scared than dead."

He had a clear view of the land and, with his gun in his hand, he felt ready for trouble. If they should be attacked, he knew he could protect Meredith.

She shrugged and headed down the steps toward a small garden off to the right. Like so many other things, he'd not seen the garden when he'd arrived four—or was it five—nights ago.

The garden sported rows of baby tomatoes, peas, carrots, potatoes and herbs divided by well-manicured paths. By summer it would be lush.

Meredith set her basket down and tugged a set of gardening gloves from her waistband. She shoved her slender hands into the fabric, working her fingers until the fit was just right. Without another glance at him, she started to pull weeds from the narrow rows between the plants.

The ranch land was rich, ablaze with spring's rebirth. A clear-water stream lined with trees flowed on the east side of the property and the west wildflowers carpeted the gently rolling land.

Meredith's hound dog meandered out from the barn toward her in the garden and sat down in the shade near her. His horse, looking fit and strong, pranced in the corral by the barn.

He relaxed in the chair and pulled the folds of his robe closed. He savored the way the sun beat down on his face. And a completely foreign sensation struck him.

He was content.

* * *

Meredith wished he'd stop staring.

Rafferty had a way of making her skin tingle when he sat silently watching her. Like a centurion, he sat straight, with his hand resting on his gun, as if he were ready to fend off any attacker.

Grateful for her garden, she dug trembling hands into the rich soil, savoring the way it felt cool and familiar against her skin. She'd never had a garden until she'd moved to Texas and she loved it.

She and her uncle had arrived early in the spring last year, time for her to plant a simple plot. The untilled land had been hard and she'd had to settle for a smaller garden. This year she'd expanded, adding rows of herbs, more carrots and even marigolds for cutting.

Next year...

There'd be no next year, Meredith reminded herself. With the new doctor arriving any day, she'd be moving into town. Mrs. Harper had offered to let her a room and there'd been talk of letting her teach school in the fall. And Mr. Walker wanted to marry her.

She almost laughed. Here she was fretting over moving back into town when she could very well find herself in prison.

A familiar tightness returned to Meredith's chest. She dug deeper into the soil, savagely attacking a stubborn weed embedded between two tomato plants.

She glanced up at Rafferty from under her bonnet. She knew so little about the man, what drove him. Before she thought, she heard herself saying, "Where'd you grow up?"

Even at twenty paces she saw Rafferty's eyes narrow. "Richmond."

She didn't hide her shock. "You did? It seemed we'd have crossed paths at one point."

He folded his arms over his chest. "Why are you asking so many questions?"

She pulled a weed. "We're here together. It only stands to reason I'd want to know more about you."

"I'm not making a social call, Meredith. There's no reason for us to get to know each other. Once our business is done, I'll be accepting a new army posting and we'll never see each other again."

She ignored the irritation in his voice. "You're still in the army? I thought you'd left."

"I had a lot of leave time coming and I took it."

Her attempt to keep the conversation light was failing. "To find me."

"Yes." He spoke with fierce resolve. He was a man who got what he went after.

Meredith refused to dwell on that, either. "I was born in Alexandria. Lovely town. Ever been there?"

He stared at her as if she was daft, then seemed to accept the fact that they were going to talk. "Yes."

"There's a wonderful tavern near the river. Brookmont's," she said.

A flicker of recognition sparked in his eyes. "I know the place."

"They have the best fried fish. But do you know what my favorite dish is?"

"I suppose you're going to tell me."

"The crab cakes. I love them." She paused, letting her mind drift. "I miss Virginia."

He leaned forward. "Then why run so far away from it?"

"When James was killed there was no more reason to stay. Uncle was sick and needed a drier climate. Trail's End offered Uncle a bonus and a house if he came here."

Rafferty backtracked. "The Carters didn't want you to stay?"

She sighed. "If I'd been carrying James's child, his mother would have invited us to stay at their estate, but there was no child. And then I refused to attend James's funeral. Mrs. Carter was furious. She tracked me down later. It was an ugly scene.''

His gaze sharpened. ''Why didn't you go to the funeral?''

''It was too painful.'' Suddenly a wall of unwanted memories crashed on her.

''You're shaking,'' he said.

She forced a smile. ''It must be chilly.''

''The sun is high. It's warm.'' He stared at her for long, tense seconds.

She sat back on her heels. ''Every time I talk about James, Virginia or the war, it brings all the sadness back. Stupid, I know, but I always seem to cry.''

He stared at the horizon so long that when he spoke, his voice startled her. ''Smells bring it back to me.'' He touched his bandage, rubbing the flesh around it as if it ached. ''The smell of gunpowder. The rusty scent of blood. They take me back to the battlefield.''

The few people in town who'd been in the war never spoke of it. Now hearing Rafferty talk about the war opened a floodgate of emotions. ''The smell of rubbing alcohol transports me back to the hospitals.''

Rafferty's fingers tightened around the arm of the rocking chair. "Nightmares?"

She rose and walked toward the porch. She stopped at the bottom step and tugged off her gloves. "Almost every night. Some nights my heart is racing so badly when I wake, I'm dizzy."

Slowly he nodded. "Bathed in sweat."

"Sick to my stomach."

Each understood. The war had left an invisible mark on them both.

"We're a fine pair, aren't we, Rafferty?"

He stared at her as if seeing her for the first time. "Yeah, a fine pair."

Chapter Seven

Talking to Rafferty had lifted Meredith's spirits. She felt better than she had in months—as if a weight had been lifted from her shoulders.

However, Rafferty looked awful. The white pallor of his face was proof he'd had enough for one day. "Time to get you inside and back into bed."

He opened his mouth ready to protest, then as if thinking better of it, rose slowly. He picked up his gun belt as she wrapped her arm around his waist. After giving her some of his weight, he allowed her to help him to his bed. She steadied him as he eased down onto the mattress.

He was breathing hard. "That took more out of me than I thought."

She fluffed his pillows, noted his scent clung

to the rough cotton. "I still need to change your bandage. Once that's done, you can sleep for a few hours."

He shook his head. "I've slept enough."

Still stubborn. "No such thing as enough when you're healing."

He eased into the pillows and sighed. "If more men come, I want to be ready."

"I'll be awake. If anyone comes, I'll get you. And you've got your guns."

His eyes drifted closed then snapped open. "I don't like any of this."

"I know." She covered him with the blankets then helped him slip out of his robe. She nodded to the bloom of red on his shoulder. "You're bleeding."

He glanced at the bandage. "Damn."

"You should have stayed in bed. I'll put a kettle on for tea and get my bag." Within minutes, she had found her doctor's bag and fresh bandages and filled the kettle with water. She laid out the clean gauze bandaging on the side table, thread for stitching and a needle.

Rafferty watched her intently but said nothing. The intensity of his stare made her insides jitter and she had to focus to keep her hand steady as she unwound the binding and peeled back the bandage. His skin was warm and rough, yet she liked the feel of it.

She inspected the wound. "Just a little tear. Nothing extra bandaging won't cure. But you're going to need some salve."

"Disappointed you can't drive that needle through me?"

The touch of humor in his voice had her smiling. "It is a pity." She mixed water and fresh herbs into a fine paste. "This will take the burn away."

He wrinkled his nose. "That's the stuff you used on Ward."

"Yes." She remembered the stench of the prison cell, the faces of the men, the young man who lay critically injured on the pallet. It would be smart not to talk of Libby Prison, to avoid upsetting the tentative bond between them. Still, she heard herself asking, "Whatever happened to him?"

He was silent for so long she thought he'd not answer. "Traded in a prisoner exchange. He spent the rest of the war recovering."

She kept her attention on his wound. "His arm?"

"Not perfect. But for the most part intact."

She slowly smoothed the thick paste into his tanned skin. "What about Murphy?"

He winced at her touch. "You remember Sergeant Murphy?"

"Tall, big man. Red hair. Nice face."

The tightness in his muscles ebbed. "That's him. He made it."

"Good. He struck me as a nice man."

"He was taken with you."

She almost laughed. "I looked like a horror that night. I'd traded my time between the hospital and uncle's bedside most of the day. My hair was plastered to my head from the melting snow."

"None of the men were looking at your hair," he said wryly.

She remembered the lean, hungry look in the men's eyes. "Oh."

"Murphy worried you wouldn't get home safely in the dark."

She'd been so scared of Rafferty that night, she'd run all the way home. "He shouldn't have worried. I went straight home."

Silent, Rafferty's eyes narrowed as if he were trying to read her thoughts. "Your uncle was sick that night."

"Yes. He nearly died."

"I only met the old man once, but I liked him. He was full of vinegar."

Thinking of her uncle since his death had always made her sad. Today, though, there were just pleasant, warm memories. "He was a good man." With her fingers, she scooped out a thick glob of paste. "If you lie back against the pillows, I'll rub this in."

His gaze didn't waver from her as he eased back. Her eyes skittered from the wound to the well-muscled contours of his body, which now seemed to engulf the bed.

She sat on the edge of the mattress and dolloped the ointment on the wound. "It may be a little cold."

"It's fine."

With trembling fingers, she gently worked in the salve. He closed his eyes, relaxing into the mattress. His face was a mixture of pleasure and pain as she worked the medicine into the inflamed area with her feather-light touch.

She liked touching him. There was always an energy that passed from his flesh to her fingertips. She took longer than she should with the salve, reasoning that she simply was taking good care of him.

When she'd finished, she wiped her hands and

reached for a clean square. "You're going to have to sit up so I can wrap the bandage."

"I nearly fell asleep." With a groan, he sat up and swung his legs over the side of the bed.

"You're exhausted." She pressed the cloth into the wound. "Can you hold this?"

His fingers brushed hers, and for an instant, held them against the soft gauze. The same jolt snapped through her fingers and she froze. She marveled at the size of his hand, which had to be twice hers. His touch was light, but there was no denying the strength and the power in his hand or in his body.

Her heart thumped hard against her chest and the heat from his body drew her closer. She dared a glance down at him and saw the vivid blue eyes staring at her. The anger was gone, replaced by something dark, smoldering. Frightening, alluring.

A deep yearning, something she could not define, uncoiled inside her.

She pulled her hand away.

Moistening dry lips, she reached for the fresh binding. She wound it under his arm, and then slashed it tightly across his chest like a pirate's sash.

She tore the edges and tied them off. "That should hold you for today."

When he didn't respond, she turned to leave. She'd go outside, breathe the fresh air.

But as she turned, he captured her hand. With his thumb he drew circles on her palm, sending shivers through her body. A gentle tug and she found herself sitting next to him on the bed.

A man had never smelled so good to her. Suddenly she was very aware of the years she'd spent living alone, her paltry experience with men, and the yearning in her that had been awakened but never satisfied by James.

"I don't like it any better than you." His voice was a hoarse whisper.

Jolted from her thoughts, she was surprised to find him staring at her. "What?"

"The pull. The attraction. I don't want it to be there, either. But you and I both know it is drawing us together."

This wasn't happening. "There's nothing between us. I took care of you, saved your life, that's all this is."

"I know the difference between gratitude and lust, Meredith. What we're feeling is lust."

He spoke with authority that had her hackles rising, but the plain truth was that he was right. "This is a complication neither of us needs."

"I know." He traced the line of her jaw with

his forefingers then slid it to the nape of her neck. He entwined his fingers in her hair and coaxed her face forward. "Maybe a taste is all we need."

Mesmerized by the sound of his voice, she leaned toward him. "We'll probably hate it."

"Probably."

He didn't sound as though he believed that for an instant. He leaned so close all she could see were his eyes and full lips.

Still she wasn't worried. Yes, she wanted the kiss more than she'd wanted anything in a very long time, but she'd been kissed before and knew what to expect. Once they'd tasted each other, the curiosity would be satisfied and they could move on.

Or so she thought.

The kiss started off tentative. He sampled and explored first. Then he teased her lips open with his tongue.

Meredith leaned into the kiss.

Heat burst inside her, spreading to her limbs and warming her. And that sobering realization jerked her back to reality. His touch was intoxicating and far too dangerous, like playing with fire. Dazzling, beautiful and very dangerous.

She stiffened and pushed him way. She nearly vaulted off the bed. Jamming her hands into her apron pocket, she backed away from the bed as if it were a den of snakes.

He sat up slowly, his eyes dark with wanting.

She touched her lips, shocked by her behavior. "That wasn't what I expected."

"No, it wasn't." He shoved his fingers through his hair. "It was better."

"Don't say that!"

He shrugged. "Like I said earlier. I don't like it any better than you."

She nearly laughed at the absurdity of it all. "A half-dozen men from town have tried to court me. I said no to them all. Mr. Walker has been hinting for weeks about marriage."

He frowned. "Lucky you."

"Lucky? The first man to touch me in years is determined to see me behind bars." She shook her head. "And I'm not sure if he even *likes* me."

Rafferty rubbed his hands together. "You sure can pick 'em, Meredith."

Later that evening, Rafferty sat by his bedroom window. Kissing Meredith had stirred the restlessness inside him. The setting sun slashed across the endless grasslands dotted with blue flowers. There was a rawness about this land that touched his soul. No scars, no pain, just fresh starts. Like unmolded clay, it was waiting to be reshaped.

The army had ceased to challenge him years ago and he'd have left by now if not for the war. He'd stayed on to see the fight through, but now that it was over, there was little to hold him beyond his commitment to the army, which ended next year.

Perhaps, after his tour, he'd move out West. He'd dreamed of ranching, owning his own land, and building instead of tearing down.

The idea lifted his spirits. Perhaps, a change of scenery and new challenges would help him rediscover the fire he'd once had in his belly.

Turning from the window, he stretched, trying to work the stiffness from his limbs. It was barely past six, but he was exhausted. The damn bullet hole and fever had drained him and, no matter how hard he willed it to be otherwise, his strength failed him.

As much as it galled him, he'd not be riding for at least a week. Meredith had been right about his recovery.

Meredith.

She'd been wrong earlier when she'd said he didn't like her. He did. With each passing hour, he had more and more trouble holding on to his hate and resentment. Like water, it was trickling through his fingers.

At every turn, her actions challenged everything. She could have let him die but didn't. She could have managed his care poorly and left him a cripple. Or let the fever take him. She hadn't done any of that.

What was she up to?

He rubbed the back of his neck with his hand. "You'll drive yourself mad, trying to figure the woman out."

Travis knew now he should never have kissed Meredith. He'd broken his number-one rule today: never get too close. Personal entanglements were messy and created unnecessary complications.

He knew that.

So why had he given in to the urge to taste her. Why did he miss her touch, her scent and her heat?

He rose and moving slowly, closed the door to his room, shrugged off his robe and tossed it on the edge of the bed. The cool air felt good against his naked skin.

He sat on the edge of the bed, leaned back and tucked his hand behind his head. His desire for Meredith was easy enough to explain. He was a healthy male who'd not had a woman in months, and Meredith was a beautiful woman.

He shoved out a sigh. Time to get a grip on his emotions. This simply was not like him.

The soft thud of Meredith's feet echoed in the cabin. She was always close, always puttering around, and the thought was oddly comforting.

Signs of her were everywhere. When the dog barked and thumped his tail against the floor, her soft laughter floated around him. He heard a cat mew and purr and she spoke. The aroma of her cooking wafted through the air.

He'd not seen her in a couple of hours and realized he missed her.

Meredith had stayed clear of him all afternoon, but that didn't diminish his awareness of her.

He couldn't shake the feel of her lips, the flush of passion in her cheeks. His body throbbed with wanting just as it had when he was a young recruit on leave.

Staring down at his erection, he groaned. If he had the strength, he'd drag himself to the cool stream out back.

"Damn," he muttered. He shoved his hands through his hair. Why couldn't Meredith be more like Isabelle, his ex-fiancée? All this would be so much easier.

The two were society bred, each growing up with all the advantages. Both were beautiful and carried themselves with poise and an elegance reserved for the wealthy.

Yet, Isabelle wouldn't have stuck by an ailing uncle or moved to the wilds of Texas with him. She'd never have dug her pretty little hands into the dirt, nor would she have fed and watered his horse or mucked out a stall.

Meredith possessed a grit and strength that he had to admire. She was a survivor.

If his begrudging admiration and desire for her wasn't enough, a possessiveness had reared its ugly head today. Her casual mention of Walker and the other suitors had made his blood boil. He didn't like the idea of her sharing her life with another man.

Suddenly there was a quick knock at the door. "I've got your dinner."

Before he could cover himself, she came into the room with a tray of food. Her gaze dropped to his naked body, his arousal. The color drained from her face.

Immediately she retreated a step. "Oh my." She turned. "I—I'm sorry to have intruded. I'm so accustomed to finding you asleep. I'll leave your dinner on the kitchen table."

He cursed and covered his erection, which now throbbed painfully. It was plain foolish to let her get under his skin like this. He'd let his guard down once for a woman and it had been a mistake.

One he didn't intend to repeat.

No, Meredith Carter was wrong for him. He had a duty to his fallen comrades. His loyalty lay with them, not Meredith Carter.

Yet he couldn't seem to stop asking the same question over and over.

What was he going to do when Meredith was gone from his life forever?

Chapter Eight

By early Friday morning Meredith realized she couldn't get away from Rafferty fast enough.

Last night, as she'd heard him pacing the living room outside her door, she'd realized how strong he'd become. In a few days he'd be riding, which meant they'd be leaving for Washington.

As quietly as she could, she dug her carpetbag out from under her bed and opened it. She'd barely spoken to Rafferty these past few days and she'd gone out of her way to avoid him. She changed his bandage daily and saw that he had plenty to eat, but otherwise she stayed clear.

There'd been no more talk of proving her innocence. No more kisses.

Tonight, after Rafferty fell asleep, she'd saddle her horse and ride toward Austin. There she'd catch the stage and head west, Colorado maybe. It would be a least a week before Rafferty could follow. Not much time but enough to lose herself in the wilderness.

She went to her bureau, dug out her blouses and shoved them into her valise. As she collected ribbons from her top dresser drawer her fingers brushed a picture frame. She picked up the picture. It was a picture of James and her taken on their wedding day.

She'd worn a white gown with a full skirt and a gossamer veil that trailed over her shoulders and down to the floor. Around her neck hung her mother's cameo. Her smile was radiant, so full of hope.

James wore his freshly pressed uniform with cuffs trimmed in silver braid, polished boots that stretched to his knees and a saber at his side.

She smoothed her fingertip over the picture. "Lord, it was a lifetime ago."

She looked into the mirror. Her hair hung loose, slightly damp from the bath she'd taken last night. Some of the color had returned to her cheeks and the circles had faded from under her eyes.

But she wasn't smiling. In fact, it seemed she never smiled anymore. She couldn't remember the last time she'd laughed.

As a girl, when James courted her, there was always laughter and the rush of excitement and that giddy feeling that left her tongue-tied. Then, she'd worn bright cottons and pretty hats. There'd been parties. Lots of friends. Life had been full of promise.

She scrutinized the shapeless white apron that hung over her worn calico dress. Somewhere along the way, she'd lost the joy of living.

Meredith made a face in the mirror. She mugged an exaggerated smile. "Stop feeling sorry for yourself."

Life may have not turned out as she'd expected, but that didn't mean she was giving up. Once Rafferty was out of her life, her world would be brighter.

She'd find a new place to live. She'd marry. Have children. Yes, once Rafferty was gone, she'd be fine.

So if everything was going to be perfect, why did she feel like crying?

"What is wrong with me?" Swallowing her grief, she shoved the picture back into the bureau, packed a few other essentials in her bag and snapped it closed.

Her decision made, she stowed her bag under her bed and moved through the cottage and to the front door. She planned to visit her uncle's grave one last time and didn't want Rafferty trailing behind her.

Their daily routine was falling into a predictable pattern. He'd rise once he heard her go outside, then he'd move to the front porch, his rifle in hand. She could never decide if he was keeping watch over her or standing guard as she moved about the compound.

Gingerly she opened the front door and closed it without a sound. With any luck, he'd not stirred yet.

Black thunderclouds blanketed the morning sky, dulling the colors of the landscape. Rain threatened. She hated traveling in the rain, but the water would wash away her tracks when she rode out tonight.

She was across the front yard and moving up the small rise toward her uncle's grave when she heard the front door open and close. Damn. She didn't need to look back to know Rafferty had taken his post on the porch, rifle in hand.

She imagined those blue eyes watching her, not missing a detail. The skin on the back of her neck tingled.

"No reason to worry," she muttered. "He has no idea you're leaving."

Meredith cleared her throat as she reached the grave under the oak tree marked by the simple stone marker. She'd not been up here in almost three weeks and, thanks to several storms, the grave was covered with sticks and brush. She knelt in front of the marker that read simply "Castleman."

She started to sweep away the leaves with her hand. "Sorry, I've not been here in so long. I've a Yank captain sleeping under my roof."

The rustle of trees was her only answer, but she could feel her nerves easing. Here she felt close to her uncle if only for a moment or two.

"His name's Rafferty. You met him in Libby Prison." She brushed the leaves from the top of the headstone. "It's a long story and I won't bore you with details, but I'm leaving. I'll be back, but I may have to be gone a good while."

Her chest tightened, and a tear trailed down her cheek. "You'd think I'd be used to moving by now."

As she lifted a thick branch with withered green leaves that lay across the grave mound, a rattling sound caught her attention. She froze and looked up. Three feet away, a rattler sat coiled, ready to strike.

The snake had set up home in the rubble by the

grave and Meredith had disturbed it. She started to draw her hand back. The snake hissed.

Meredith swallowed. "Nice snake," she whispered.

The rattler shook its tail and readied itself to strike. Time slowed to a crawl. A bead of sweat trickled down her spine. She could count each of her heartbeats.

"Don't move." Rafferty's voice was full of quiet command.

Tears welled in Meredith's eyes. She'd never thought she'd be glad to hear his voice. "What do I do?" she whispered.

"Stay still." He cocked his pistol.

She didn't dare lift her gaze to his, fearing she'd start to cry. She tried to remember a prayer her uncle had taught her as a child, but before she could utter the first word, Rafferty fired.

Meredith flinched and the snake jerked violently back.

His pistol still trained on the reptile, he moved forward. Despite his injury, his stride was even. He poked the dead snake with the tip of his gun barrel and only when he was satisfied it was dead, did he relax.

He grabbed the snake by its rattler. "I'd say he was five feet long."

Meredith shrank onto her heels and released the breath she'd been holding. "The warm days must have stirred him."

"Likely." He held the snake out to her. "You eat rattler?"

She held up her hands to ward off the snake. "No!"

"I never had much of a taste for it, either. But some animal will." Rafferty moved down the hill toward a thicket near the river. Then in one smooth move, he tossed the snake into the woods.

Meredith rose. Her hands were trembling and, despite the cool morning air, sweat dampened her back. Rafferty strode back up the hill to her.

He'd hastily dressed but left the top button of his pants unfastened. His white bandage accentuated the deep, rich color of his skin and the curls on his chest. His hair stuck up in wild spikes and dark stubble blanketed his square chin. Her mouth started to water. "Thanks."

He dragged his hand through his hair. "Anybody ever tell you not to put your hands into brush?"

Her uncle had said the same thing a hundred times. Still, coming from Rafferty, it irritated. "I wasn't thinking."

Rafferty glanced at the gravestone. His expression softened. "Out here, if you don't think, you die."

She raised her chin. "I've managed so far just fine without you."

"Yeah, you're doing a hell of a job." He surveyed the horizon, always alert to danger. Muttering another oath, he took her elbow and started back to the cabin. "Let's get out of the open."

"Do you always look for trouble?"

"Where you're concerned, yes."

"You saved my life once—twice—in the past week. But I never had a problem until *you* showed up," she said as she hurried to match his pace. "I think you just bring trouble with you."

He cocked an eyebrow. "*I* bring trouble?"

She noted that the top of her head barely reached his shoulder. "I don't think you mean to," she hurried to say. "Some folks just attract it."

"You should know." They climbed the front steps and he opened the front door, waited until she walked inside and then closed the door. Shielded now by the house, he relaxed.

"Do me a small favor. Stay inside at least until I get dressed. That way the next time I have to save your pretty little hide, I'll have my pants fastened properly."

She pouted. "You make me sound like a child."

He laid his hands on her shoulders. "Promise."

She saluted. "Not going anywhere, Captain."

"Good." He took his pistol with him and retreated to his bedroom.

She moved into the kitchen. As she reached for the coffeepot on the stove, she realized her hands were trembling. The sound of the rattler's tail echoed in her ears. Her knees went weak, forcing her to sit in the chair. Breathing slowly, she tried not to think about how close she'd come to being bitten.

Rafferty had been right. She hadn't been thinking clearly at the grave. She'd been thinking about running from him, not the dangers right in front of her nose. She'd have to be more careful.

The sound of shattering glass echoed through the cabin. "Damn it!" Rafferty's voice boomed like a roar.

She hurried to Rafferty's bedroom door, reached for the handle and stopped. Memories of him standing naked and so...*there* flashed in her mind. "Rafferty. Are you all right?"

"Yes," he growled.

"Can I come in?"

"Why not."

She found him sitting on his bed. He'd been trying to put on his shirt and in the process had knocked the water glass off the table by his bed.

He glared at the shirt, balled up in his hand now as if it had personally offended him. "I can't get it over my head."

"You just climbed a hill and saved me from a rattler."

Irked, he tossed the shirt onto the bed. "This requires more dexterity. My stitches are pulling."

Without waiting for his permission, she took the shirt from him and fluffed the wrinkles out of it. "That's because they're healing. They should be ready to come out tomorrow." She worked her hands through the collarless neck opening. "May I?"

He nodded his acceptance, this time not questioning her help.

She pulled the shirt over his head and waited patiently as he carefully worked his good arm then his injured arm through the sleeve.

When she reached for the buttons, he pushed her hand away. "I'll do it."

To her surprise, he deftly fastened the buttons with one hand. He looked up at her with triumph in his eyes.

"Bravo," she said.

"Didn't think I could do it, did you?"

"No. But I never would have thought you could climb that hill or shoot a rattler, either. You're full of surprises."

Pleased, he nodded. "Don't forget it."

He was nearly back to his old self. For the first time, she worried that she'd waited too long to leave. Escaping him might not be so easy now. Maybe she should have left days ago. "You're healing faster than I'd expected."

He tucked in his shirt then laced up his boots. "Disappointed?"

"Of course not." She frowned.

"You look a little pale."

"The snake scared me." She retreated, needing distance. "I'll get breakfast."

Without waiting for his response, she left the room. The scent of coffee wafted from the pot she'd set on the stove to brew when she'd first awakened. She shoved extra kindling into the stove's firebox, stoking it until it blazed. After setting her big fry skillet on the stovetop, she sliced ham and laid it in the pan.

As the ham cracked and popped, she couldn't help but fret. She didn't want to leave her home or friends.

She heard Rafferty move slowly into the kitchen, but didn't turn around as he sniffed.

"Is that coffee?" he said, his voice little more than a rasp.

She removed a cup from the shelf above the stove and filled it with the brew. She set it in front of him.

He sipped the coffee. "It's good."

Nodding, Meredith turned back to her ham. As it sizzled, she cracked five eggs into a bowl and started to scramble them.

"In the field, the coffee we had tasted like mud. Thick, black, half the time it was more bark or chicory than coffee. If it hadn't been hot, I doubt any sane man would have drunk it."

Suddenly this whole moment struck her as insane. She was cooking breakfast for a man who was taking her to prison.

She turned, a wood spoon in her hand. "Why are you telling me this?" Thick stubble blanketed his square jaw, giving him the look of a renegade.

He shrugged. "Making conversation."

"Why? You're taking me away from my life, back to Washington. If you had your way, I'll spend the next fifteen years in jail."

He set his cup down. "I've been thinking about that the past couple of days."

She cocked an eyebrow.

He cleared his throat. "I owe you for saving my life."

She made no effort to hide her irritation. "You don't owe me a thing. In fact, I owe you. You saved me twice."

He tapped his finger on the cup. "I'm not very good at changing directions. Once my mind is set I rarely deviate. But I've had time to think while I've been healing. There were too many times you could have walked away and left me. You didn't. The least I can do is consider other suspects."

A rush of relief flooded her senses at the small victory and she couldn't hold on to her anger. "You really mean that?"

"Yeah," he said, setting the cup on the table. "We're stuck here together for a while longer. We'll spend the time going over that last day in Libby."

Unreasonably happy, Meredith hugged him. "Thank you!"

He flinched. "Don't hug so tight."

Immediately she drew back. "I'm sorry! Did I hurt you?"

He rubbed his tender shoulder, testing. "No worse for the wear. Any other time I wouldn't have minded."

Color flooded her cheeks. His voice held a seductive quality that warmed her. "I'd hate to undo days of healing."

He stared at her a long, silent moment as if seeing her for the first time. The taste of cotton in her mouth, she stood close to him, not able to step away.

She was as giddy as a schoolgirl. It felt good to smile.

"You won't be sorry you helped me. You'll see that I'm right."

"I'm not making any promises."

"Just keep an open mind."

Her skin prickled as he stared at her. She had the urge to kiss him.

Foolish. Foolish. Foolish.

"Sit down," she said, keeping her voice breezy. "I'll finish your breakfast."

He lingered a beat longer, then nodded and took his seat at the table.

Meredith removed the ham and placed it on two tin plates. She whisked the eggs and dropped them into the pan. After stirring them until they were thoroughly scrambled, she then set them next to the ham on their plates.

She set the food on the table, along with napkins and utensils. "Where do you want to start on your investigation?"

He sipped his coffee. "The prison guard in Richmond. His testimony was the most damning."

She took her seat at the table. "Spider. I remember him. How will you get him to talk?"

"I can be persuasive."

Meredith laughed. "I'll bet." They slipped into an easy silence as they ate. For the first time in weeks, she felt as if a weight had been lifted off her shoulders. Maybe, just maybe, it would all work out for the best.

"You were up early this morning," he said. "Before dawn."

Alert, she pushed the food around on her plate. "I had a lot to do. With the extra animals, there's more work." Lying didn't sit well with her.

"Spring cleaning, too?"

"What?"

His tone was casual. "Sounded like you were opening and closing dresser drawers."

"I was pulling out summer-weight dresses." She stabbed a piece of ham but didn't eat it. "It gets real hot here in the summer."

He chewed his food thoughtfully. "It does get hot down here."

A knot coiled in her stomach. "Yeah."

When he'd finished his meal, he tossed his napkin on the table. "I've got questions for you about that night in Libby."

"I'll tell you everything I know."

"Great. We'll start as soon as you unpack that bag you got stowed under your bed."

Chapter Nine

"Bag?" Meredith coughed, trying not to look guilty. "What are you talking about?"

Travis nearly laughed as he watched the play of emotions on Meredith's face. Shock. Outrage. He sipped his coffee. "The carpetbag. The one stuffed so full it's barely staying closed."

"Oh, *that* one." Meredith rose and picked up their plates. She frowned as if giving the matter great thought. "It's just full of old blankets and sheets."

"Give it up, Meredith. You were planning to ditch me tonight."

Carefully she laid their plates in the sink. "I don't know what you're talking about."

He leaned back in his chair, comfortable. She was a bad liar. "You were planning on leaving me."

She kept her gaze averted. "If I were going to leave you, I would have done it by now. Besides, it's going to rain."

"You didn't want to leave me until you were sure I could take care of myself. We both know I can now." Her loyalty pleased him.

A week ago, he'd been so sure of her betrayal. Now he wasn't certain of anything.

She shrugged. "You said you'd help me. Why would I run?"

"I only just agreed to help," he pointed out. "When you woke this morning, you knew we'd be leaving for Washington in a day or two."

She frowned, as if searching for a retort. She couldn't find one and apparently settled on the truth. "Yes, I was going to leave. But you have to admit, you haven't been very reasonable."

Her logic caught him off guard. "I've been very reasonable. I am going to help you, aren't I?"

She shot him a glance over her shoulder as she washed the dishes. "Yes, now. Until this moment, though, you were like a runaway train. There was no changing your course."

He sipped his coffee to hide his smile. How many times had a commanding officer told him the same? "Being focused has kept me on course."

"Bullheaded," she mumbled.

To his surprise, he was enjoying himself. The banter exhilarated him. He'd never talked to Isabelle like this and he'd certainly never talked with his men or commanding officers with such familiarity. A man could get used to having Meredith around.

Travis set down his cup, annoyed at the direction of his thoughts. Any kind of relationship between them was impossible. He understood that, accepted it. Yet, he still wanted her naked and under him.

So why the connection? He couldn't muster an ounce of logic to explain it, but like it or not, it was there.

Drying her hands, Meredith set a kettle on the stove. "Bullheaded is also a good quality. I'm going to need tenacity to get out of this mess."

"Then you've come to the right place."

A smile tugged the edges of her lips. "Now that you're on my side, I'm not so afraid of returning to Washington."

My side. She spoke the words so casually, yet they rang in his head like a church bell. Pleased and irritated that she'd given him her trust so freely, he shifted.

She set two mugs on the table and sprinkled tea leaves in them. "It's hard to believe it's been two years since I've been to Washington. I thought I'd never see it again. Has it changed much?"

"No."

"What was playing at the theater before you left? James and I loved to see plays there."

A comedy, he thought, but he wasn't sure. "I don't pay much attention to that."

She sighed. "When we first moved to Texas, I missed the people, the buzz of activity so much. Now I love the quiet, the open spaces."

"It still has too many people."

"I doubt I'd recognize the place. Or know how to act there anymore." She studied the calluses on her palm. Worry flashed in her green eyes.

She'd gone from fancy parlors to a run-down cabin and she'd managed just fine. "You are a survivor. You'll adapt."

She grinned. "I'm not so sure that's a compliment from you."

He liked seeing her smile. "An observation."

She poured the hot water into the cups and let it steep as she moved into the main room. From a chest near the fire she pulled out a wooden box and opened it. Chess pieces were jumbled inside. "Do you play?"

He picked up the mugs and followed. "It's been a while. Are you any good?"

Her eyes sparkled as she pulled a small table in front of his chair. "Very good."

His blood warmed to the challenge. "Not as good as I am."

Her throaty laugh was oddly seductive as she laid out the board. "Uncle taught me, then regretted ever doing it. I was forever begging him for a game."

Raindrops began to pelt the roof. It was cold and gray outside, but Meredith's cabin was warm and cozy.

Travis set the mugs down on the table and took a seat. He started to line up the black pieces. The last piece, the queen, he held on to as he spoke. "You won't be begging me for another game once I've beaten you."

She pulled her chair closer to her board. "So confident. Sure you don't want the white pieces and the first move?"

"Positive. You'll need the advantage."

"You may eat those words."

He laughed, enjoying himself for the first time in many years.

She dropped her gaze to the board and her brow furrowed. She moved her center pawn two spaces forward. "Are you afraid yet?"

"Terrified." He moved his center pawn two spaces forward. It would be easy to savor the moment and simply enjoy her company. But he couldn't ignore why he'd come to Texas. The dead cried for justice and until they knew peace, he never would. "Tell me about that night."

She paused, her rook clasped between her fingers. "After I left you at the prison?"

"Yes."

She set the rook back in its original place and leaned back in her chair. Drawing in a breath, she forcibly relaxed her shoulders. "As I said, after I left you that night, I started home. It was too late and too cold to make any other calls."

He flexed the fingers of his right hand into a fist, and then relaxed them. "You should never have gone to the prison alone. That was stupid."

"So you keep telling me."

"I'm surprised your husband let you go out." His jealousy surprised him. In all the years he'd been with Isabelle, he'd never been jealous.

"James wasn't in Richmond. He and his men had left days before."

"What happened next?"

"After I checked on my uncle, I couldn't sleep, so I got a book and sat by the fire in my bedroom." She cleared her throat. "But I must have fallen asleep in the chair. The next thing I remember was the alarm bells. They woke me."

Travis picked up a pawn. He'd heard the same sounds in his dreams every night for the past two years. "Just after midnight."

"Twelve forty-two to be precise. I can still hear the bells clanging, the men shouting, the dogs barking. It was dreadful."

"The moon had been bright that night."

"Thousands of stars in the sky," she whispered. "The next morning I went back to the prison."

His brain sharpened. "Why?" The guard he'd interviewed said she'd never come back.

"I came to check on Lieutenant Ward, but he was gone. The guards had released him."

An uneasy feeling gnawed at his gut. "Are you sure Ward was gone?"

"Yes, I'm quite sure. I had a salve for him."

"Ward said he stayed at the prison another week. He wasn't exchanged until the first of March." He tapped the top of a pawn. "Did the guards tell you where he was? Maybe they moved him to another floor."

"No, they released him."

The muscles in the back of his neck tightened as they did when facts didn't add up. "Why'd they let him go?" he said more to himself.

"Perhaps they took pity on him."

A bitter smile tipped the corner of his mouth. "Pity had nothing to do with it. The guards hated Ward."

"Why?"

"I never really found out. I cared more about the tunnel than his problems with the guards." He shook his head. "Nothing you say corroborates what Ward told me."

"I'm not lying," she said clearly.

"I didn't say you were."

"But Ward is a captain in the United States army." She paused, drew in a breath. "He has no reason to lie, whereas I have every reason."

"All true."

She was quiet for a long moment. "Do you think you could ever believe me?"

The urgency in her voice drew him to his feet. "I want to."

The need to touch her suddenly overwhelmed him. She looked so vulnerable, so afraid. He stepped around the table and pulled her to her feet, laying his hand on her shoulder. To his surprise, she didn't pull away, but placed her hand over his. They stood silent, the tap of the raindrops against the roof mingling with the crackle of the fire. They were cocooned in their own world.

Green eyes stared up at him and he forgot all the good reasons why he shouldn't kiss her. He could feel her heat, and his body throbbed with wanting like never before.

She touched his chest. His heart pounded hard against her fingertips. A flurry of sensations rushed through him, almost as if he'd awakened from a long sleep.

"We are all wrong for each other," she whispered.

He cupped her chin in his hand. The feel of her soft skin made his blood burn. "I know."

She closed her eyes. "It's been so long since a man has held me in his arms. I've missed being touched."

She was talking about James, of course. Foolish to resent a dead man, but he did. He refused to be a substitute.

He tipped her head back. "Open your eyes."

Her eyes opened. They glistened with desire.

A rush of pride flooded his senses. "I want you. But I won't lie to get you. What's happening between us is about need.'' If he kept saying it, maybe he'd believe it, too.

"I know."

"I'm no fancy gentleman."

"I know who you are."

"Do you?"

"Yes."

"Say my name." He needed to hear it. Needed proof that she knew who was going to make love to her.

"Travis," she whispered.

"You can stop this right now. Just one word and I'll stop." *Run while you can.*

Silent, she stared at him. She didn't move away, but fisted his shirt in her hands. Her eyes were dark with emotion.

He'd tried to be noble, and he'd not ask a second time. He wanted her too much. "Time's up." *No more running.*

He traced her lips with his finger, savoring her softness. He had never dreamed he'd ever really touch her and he wanted to enjoy every sensation.

Travis cupped her breast through the layers of fabric and corset. The soft peaks hardened in response. "So lovely."

Her eyelids drooped lazily and she moistened her lips. "I've never felt like this before."

His rough hand slid down her narrow waist and caressed her buttocks. "Good."

Her hand slid over his flat belly. He sucked in a breath and lowered his mouth to the hollow of her neck. She inhaled a shuddering breath.

Travis knew himself well enough. He wasn't the kind of man who could love. He was a loner. A man who didn't need anyone. "No promises, Meredith."

She laid her fingers over his lips, silencing him. "I don't want promises."

His body hummed and he closed his hand over her breast and squeezed. She arched and a soft moan escaped her lips. Bursts of desire ricocheted in his body.

A loud, thundering knock on the front door shattered the moment. Rafferty tensed and immediately stepped back from Meredith. Still dazed with desire, she smoothed a shaky hand over her hip. "Who could that be?"

Rafferty reached for his pistol by the rocker. In an instant he changed from the tender lover to the warrior. "I'm shooting first and talking second."

For Meredith, it was a struggle to concentrate. Her body was still throbbing from his touch and unsatisfied need. "It could be a patient."

He pulled her behind him. "Like last time?"

The thought of more gunmen sobered her desire like a cold bucket of water. "Do you think it's trouble?"

"Until I know otherwise, I always assume it's trouble."

She followed him to the window. Rafferty drew back the curtains. The rain outside tapped against the glass.

Meredith could see a man dressed in black. Water dripped from a big floppy hat onto clothes that were already soaked. He pounded on the door again. "Meredith Carter, are you home?"

The stranger shivered and danced in place trying to keep warm, but Meredith couldn't place the sound of his voice.

"Do you know who it is?" Rafferty asked.

"I can't tell."

Rafferty moved to the door. "Stay there."

Meredith moved out of the potential line of fire. "What are you going to do?"

He reached for the latch on the door and cocked his pistol.

A breeze drifted under the front door, cooling the air around it. "Be careful."

His gaze captured hers for an instant. "Always."

Rafferty flipped the latch up, then wrapped his

long fingers around the doorknob and yanked the door open in one violent motion. "What the hell do you want?"

When the man stumbled back, nearly falling off the front porch, he reached for a rusted six-shooter tucked in his belt. "W-who the devil are you?"

Rafferty fired his pistol, knocking the stranger's gun from his shaking hand. "I'll ask the questions. Who the hell are you?"

The man looked up, clearly shocked beyond reason and unable to speak.

Meredith recognized the man and moved in front of Rafferty's gun. "His name's Nathan Miller. His wife is expecting a baby."

Nathan gulped. "You all right, Miss Meredith?"

"Yes, I'm fine."

His nose was red from the cold. "Who's this fellow?"

"This is Captain Rafferty." She motioned for Rafferty to put down his gun. He hesitated then complied.

Nathan's eyes narrowed. "What's he doing here?"

"Captain Rafferty is a patient."

Nathan glared at Rafferty. "He looks fit enough

to me. You shouldn't be having a strange man in your home.''

Meredith tried to smile. ''I had no choice, he was shot last week.'' She glanced back at Rafferty, who hadn't holstered his gun. ''Is Jenny in labor?''

Nathan shook his head as if he just remembered why he'd come. ''Yes. She's been in bed all day.''

''Her water broke?'' Mentally she ran through the list of supplies she'd need.

His shrugged his narrow shoulders. ''I think. But I ain't sure.''

Nathan was a good man, but she suspected he'd be little or no help with the delivery. ''I'll get my bag.'' With no other thought than getting to Jenny, she moved past Rafferty.

Rafferty followed Meredith into the kitchen. ''I'm not letting you just waltz out of here.''

She pulled her bag from the shelf, snapped it open and examined its contents. ''I don't have time for this.''

''Make time.''

She closed the bag. ''I've no choice. Jenny lost her last two babies. She's terrified she'll lose this one. I've got to go to her.''

Rafferty studied her an extra beat before he

shoved his gun into his holster. He reached for his coat hanging neatly on the peg by the stove. "*All right.* But I'm going with you."

She rolled her eyes as if praying for patience. "The last thing I need is another man underfoot while I deliver a baby."

He shook his head. "You'll never know I'm there. I'll be as quiet as a mouse."

She always knew when he was close. "There's no sense in you going. Babies can take a long time and you certainly don't want to be up all night."

He reached for his hat and duster. "Angel, where you go, I go."

Chapter Ten

The rain slowed them down. The ride to the Millers' ranch took longer than they'd expected and, by the time they arrived at the single cabin centered on a patch of grassland, all three of them were soaked to the bone.

Rafferty's shoulder ached, but riding had done him a world of good. His stiff muscles had loosened and he was starting to feel more like himself again. In a day or two he and Meredith could leave.

The realization didn't please him as he thought it would. A week ago, he'd had a clear vision of his goals. Arrest Meredith Carter. Move on with his life. Now nothing was clear.

He still couldn't quite believe that they'd kissed. Kissed. Who was he kidding? He'd been ready to take her right there in front of the fireplace. He'd not given a tinker's damn about consequences or honor. There had only been the driving need to have her. A need he'd barely been able to control.

Worse still, he was starting to notice things about her, like the sprinkling of freckles across the bridge of her nose and the faint wrinkle that creased her brow when she frowned. She had slender wrists, small hands and a sparkle in her eyes when that hound dog of hers barked for his supper.

None of this was good, in and of itself, but his actions today were the icing on the cake.

He was falling fast for Meredith Carter.

And he didn't know how to stop it.

After tethering the horses under a stand of trees, Rafferty trailed behind Meredith into the simple cabin lit by a handful of lanterns. The one-room cabin was small, but simple checked curtains and handmade furniture made it cozy. A fire blazed in the potbellied stove.

The right corner of the room was partitioned off with a well-worn quilt. He guessed the bed was on the other side of the curtain, judging by the soft moans of the woman who must be Nathan's wife.

Nathan opened the door of the stove and stoked the glowing embers. "I got Miss Meredith, honey," he said loudly. "It's gonna be fine now."

"Thank God." The woman's voice drifted from the other side of the blanket. She sounded weak, exhausted.

Meredith shrugged off her wet coat, handed it to Rafferty and wiped the rain from her eyes. "I don't know how long I'll be."

He automatically searched the rear of the cabin for another exit. Except for one narrow window, there was none. "Take as long as you need."

Meredith followed his line of sight and raised an eyebrow. "You're welcome to join me, though it has been my experience that men don't do so well at birthings."

She was right. He wanted no part of the birthing. Satisfied that he blocked the only way in and out of the cabin, he shrugged off his coat. "I'll wait here."

He hung their coats up by the door and moved to the fire to stand by Nathan. He held out his hands, not so sure what to say. He settled on saying nothing.

Nathan shoved his long fingers into his pockets

then pulled them out and planted them on his bony hips. He paced. He sat. Paced again.

Finally, the farmer took a deep breath. "I'd give anything to have something to do right now. But with that blasted rain, there ain't much I can do but stew."

So true.

Rafferty settled in a chair. The men lapsed into another uneasy silence as the minutes ticked away.

He could hear Meredith's voice as she spoke to Nathan's wife. Jenny, he remembered. Meredith's tone was low and soothing. She'd taken the same tone with him when the fever had raged through his body. There'd been times when the pain had been so bad that he'd clung to the sound of her voice like a lifeline.

Jenny moaned loudly, then screamed. Nathan's head shot up and he paled. "Oh, damn."

Rafferty took pity on the father-to-be. "Your wife is lucky to have Mrs. Carter at her side."

Nathan sniffed, grateful for the distraction of conversation. "I know Miss Meredith will do all she can for Jenny. It's just that my wife lost our first two babies. She's so worried about this one."

Rafferty wanted to tell him that everything would be fine, but the truth was he had no first-hand experience with this sort of thing. Fellow officers about to become fathers had been far away from the birthing of their children. They had received word in a letter from their wives, weeks after the birthing.

I'm pleased to tell you that you have a son…our daughter was small and didn't live past the second day.

"Meredith will take care of her."

Nathan swallowed. "I know she'll do her best. Likely, she's delivered hundreds of babies." He started to pace again. "You known Miss Meredith long?"

He understood Nathan needed to escape his worries and lose himself in a conversation. "A couple of years."

He looked surprised. "That's a good while."

"Yep."

Nathan folded his arms. "Meredith said you was shot."

Rafferty's jaw tightened. "That's right."

The rancher raised pencil-thin eyebrows. "You know who shot you?"

"Nope."

Nathan frowned. "You some kind of outlaw?"

"Captain. U.S. army."

"Federal?"

"Yep."

He glared at Rafferty. "I reckon that's a sight better than an outlaw. What you doing out this way?"

"I've business with Miss Meredith."

Nathan hooked his thumbs in his suspenders and puffed out his chest. "I don't know if I like the sound of that. Can't think what kind of business a Yank would have with her."

Rafferty didn't like the line of conversation.

Nathan opened his mouth, ready to follow up with another question, when Jenny screamed again. Whatever had been on the farmer's mind was forgotten. He sank into the rocker by the hearth.

Meredith appeared at the curtain opening, wiping her hands on a clean cloth. Her gown and hair were still wet and she looked chilled, but she didn't seem to notice, either. Her face had paled and was tight with worry. "Nathan," Meredith said in a calm voice that belied her expression. "I'm going to need a little help here."

Nathan's legs wobbled. "What do you need my help for?"

"I need you to help Jenny into a sitting position."

His face flushed bright red, and he headed for

the quilted partition as if he were anticipating a firing squad. "I don't know what I can do for you. I don't know the first thing about this. It's a woman's business."

She took him by the hand. "It's your child so it's your business."

Nathan glanced back at Rafferty, his eyes pleading. "Maybe the Yank could help, too. I bet he's got the stomach for this."

Rafferty's gut turned. "I'm here if you need me."

Relief washed over Nathan's face. "Bless you."

Meredith shook her head. "Jenny needs *you,* Nathan, not a stranger." She pulled the rancher behind the curtain.

Rafferty said a word of thanks. He'd always been able to push his feelings aside—do the unpleasant tasks—but this was far out of his domain. He'd barely settled in the chair, when he heard a loud thump and a crash.

Meredith cursed. "Nathan!"

Rafferty, his hand on his pistol, jumped to his feet and ran. He wasn't sure what he expected to find. Attackers and intruders he could have dealt with—he knew what to do with them. Instead he found real trouble.

Nathan lay on the floor by the wood-frame bed, passed out. A knot was already rising on his forehead and turning blue. In the center of the bed, Jenny lay on her side, her legs drawn up. Her face was ashen. She wore only a threadbare nightgown that was pushed up over her naked, swollen body. She gripped her belly as a spasm shook her body.

Instinctively he dropped his gaze. "Excuse me."

Meredith muttered an unladylike oath. "Rafferty, drag Nathan into the main room. And get back here."

Rafferty didn't argue and did as she asked. He shrugged off his jacket and rolled up his sleeves. Nothing was going his way these days.

"Is Nathan all right?" Jenny asked.

Meredith rolled Jenny onto her back. "He'll live." She looked up at Rafferty. "Jenny started to have another contraction and he fainted. My concern now is Jenny and the baby."

For the first time, Rafferty really looked at the woman. She had red hair, skin as pale as the moon and a round face that he imagined wasn't in so much pain.

Jenny's breathing was hard and fast. She gritted her teeth until the contraction subsided. "Nathan never did have the stomach for sick folks."

Meredith patted Jenny on the arm. "I heard Nathan fainted when the blacksmith smashed *his* own thumb with an anvil."

Jenny's eyes were closed, but she laughed. "Poor Steve nearly crushed his thumb, but Nathan was doing all the howling."

"That was funny." Meredith wasn't smiling when she met Rafferty's gaze. "Get behind her. She'll be having another contraction any second. When the pain starts, push her into a seated position. I need to reach inside and make sure the child is turned right."

Rafferty placed himself behind Jenny's head and slid his arms under hers. "Sorry for the intrusion, ma'am. I know this is meant to be private."

Jenny gritted her teeth as another spasm washed over her. "Right now you could be Satan for all I care."

He'd seen this kind of agony in wounded men on the battlefield. Dignity and honor were forgotten when pain ravaged the body.

Meredith, her face a mask of worry, reached inside the woman. "Hang in there."

Rafferty tightened his hold. The initial awkwardness forgotten, he found himself focused on the miracle that was about to happen. He'd seen so many men die, but he'd never seen a new life come into the world.

Meredith met Rafferty's gaze. For the first time, he saw fear. "Jenny, I'm gonna just ease the baby over. He's got himself turned around."

Jenny's contraction eased and she relaxed into Rafferty's arm. "Am I going to lose my baby?"

"No," Meredith said with conviction. "But the delivery's a little more complicated. The next time the pain comes, do *not* push."

"I don't think I can do it," Jenny whimpered. "I'm so tired. And it hurts."

Rafferty lifted her and took her hands in his. "Yes, you can, Jenny. You've just got to be determined. Remember the baby."

Meredith nodded. "The captain never takes no for an answer."

Jenny barely had time to respond before the next contraction came. "I need to push."

"Hold on," Rafferty commanded. "The longer you hold out the faster your baby will be here."

"I c-can't," Jenny whimpered.

"You can!" he said, his voice urgent.

As he coached the woman, Meredith slipped her hands inside Jenny and turned the baby. Jenny screamed, but Meredith kept her focus.

"The baby's turned," Meredith finally said.

She wiped her forehead with the back of her hand, now covered with Jenny's blood. The contraction stopped for just a few seconds before another came on its heel. ''Next time you feel like pushing, Jenny, give it all you've got.''

Jenny squeezed Rafferty's fingers so hard he thought they'd snap. His shoulder burned but he lifted the woman higher.

Jenny screamed.

''Push!'' Meredith commanded.

Jenny Miller bored down and dug deep for strength. The veins in her neck bulged.

He wondered how much more she could take, when he saw the babe's head. It was covered in blood, but he could see the child had a full head of black hair.

As the baby's face emerged, Meredith quickly wiped the inside of the child's mouth with the cloth she'd kept slung over her shoulder. ''One more push, Jenny, and your baby will be here.''

A miracle. Rafferty tore his gaze from the new baby's face. ''Come on, Jenny. You're almost there. This time tomorrow you'll be holding your child. All this will be behind you.''

Jenny nodded and pushed. The baby's shoulders slid out, followed quickly by the rest of its tiny body.

Rafferty watched in awe as Meredith turned the baby on its side, then balancing the child face-down against her forearm, she started to rub it on the back.

"Come on, little fellow. I need a big breath."

The babe lay still, its slate-gray skin a sharp contrast to Meredith's pale arm. Rafferty lowered Jenny back against the pillow. The woman's eyes were open now and trained on her baby.

Meredith thumped the baby between the shoulder blades. Nothing.

"Is it dead?" Jenny choked. "Oh Lord, I can't lose another one."

"Be calm, Jenny." Rafferty noticed that Meredith's hands, steady until now, had started to tremble.

He moved to Meredith's side and whispered. "What's wrong?"

She rubbed the child between the shoulder blades. "He needs to breathe."

Rafferty stared at the babe, willing it to breathe. When nothing happened, he took the very still, slippery child in his hand and turned it over so that it faced the floor. He smacked the child firmly on the bottom. The child inhaled a sharp breath and then let out a very loud, angry cry.

Jenny started to whimper. "Thank the Lord."

Tears glistened in Meredith's eyes.

Rafferty swallowed, his own throat tight with emotion. He turned the howling babe over, marveling how it fit in the palm of his hand. So small, so perfect.

"Is it a boy or girl?" Jenny asked

Both Rafferty and Meredith laughed. "I don't know," they said together as they checked. Then again in unison, "A boy!"

Jenny sniffed. "As stubborn and slow as his pa, no doubt."

Meredith tied off the cord and concentrated on delivering the afterbirth.

Rafferty wrapped the infant in a blanket, then cradled the child in his arms until it quieted. He marveled at the child's small fingers and toes before he laid it in Jenny's arms.

Nathan staggered into the room. "Jenny, I'm here for you, darlin'."

"Reckon, you're a little late," Jenny said tartly. She didn't look up from her son's face as she counted his fingers and toes.

Nathan rubbed the knot on his head. "Did I miss the birthing?"

Jenny's face warmed when she saw the pained expression on her husband's face. "No, darlin', you're just in time."

Now that the drama of the moment had passed, Rafferty felt like the interloper again. He moved away from the bed, ready to leave.

"Where you going?" Nathan asked. "You're as much a part of this as anybody."

"This is private," Travis countered.

"If it weren't for you, this little fellow might not have made it," Jenny said. "I reckon that makes you family now."

Travis held his ground for a moment. He'd always been an outsider. But he was amazed how good it felt to be a part of this moment.

Jenny looked up at Meredith, her eyes filled with gratitude. "Want to hold him?"

Meredith wiped her hands clean on her apron. "Thought you'd never ask."

She took the baby from Jenny and cradled it in her arms. The child relaxed into the nook of her arm. The furrow in the babe's brow eased.

The child wasn't Meredith's, but Travis saw how her expression softened, the wave of protectiveness that washed over her. She'd make a fine mother one day.

Jenny winced as she shifted. Her gaze skittered between Rafferty and Meredith. "Time you had a young'un yourself, Meredith."

Color rose in Meredith's face. "I'd expected to have one or two children by now."

Jenny giggled. "Captain, you have any children?"

He shifted, uneasy. "No."

"A man your age should have children," she said.

A family, children, had been a dream once. "I doubt children are in the cards for me."

Meredith looked up at him. She didn't speak but there was sadness in her eyes.

Jenny kept her voice even. "That's too bad. Miss Meredith, I know Mr. Walker would be happy to give you a houseful of young'uns if you would say yes."

She tore her gaze from Travis. "I know."

Jealousy snapped through Travis's veins. The idea of Walker giving Meredith babies enraged him.

Nathan coughed as if sensing Rafferty's mood shift. "Captain, we know you are a Yank, but we're still mighty beholden to you. Hard to believe, but I don't know your first name."

"Travis."

Nathan and Jenny exchanged glances, not needing words to communicate.

"Mind if we name the boy after you?" Nathan asked.

Rafferty lifted his gaze, unreasonably touched. "Meredith should name the boy. She's the one that got him here."

Nathan shifted and looked at the infant in Meredith's arms. "That would be fine as long as it ain't Ezra. My boy don't look like an Ezra to me."

Meredith laughed and moved closer to him. "Uncle was never so fond of it himself." She traced the baby's forehead with her fingertip. "I think Travis would be a better name."

Touched beyond words, Rafferty stared at Meredith. "Are you sure?"

"Travis," Jenny said, testing the name. "Yes, I like it."

Nathan nodded. "Sounds good to me."

The baby yawned as if names just didn't matter.

Meredith cleared her throat. "We best hand this little fellow back to his ma. He'll be hungry soon."

Meredith gently laid the babe in Jenny's arms.

Jenny tucked the baby's blanket closer to his chin. "We can't thank you two enough for saving little Travis here." Tears pooled in her tired brown eyes. "I couldn't have lost another."

Meredith squeezed Jenny's hand. "All's well. Don't worry." She reached for her bag. "Now let me finish up here and we'll leave you new parents alone."

Rafferty reluctantly retreated from the cabin to the front porch. The rain had stopped and the air smelled fresh and new. The sun peeked out through the clouds, glistening on the puddles. A gentle, moist breeze skimmed the tops of the grass.

He sucked in a deep breath and leaned against the porch post. Lord, but he felt good.

He stared at his hands, roughened by years of hard work. Hands that had killed. Now hands that had helped bring new life into the world.

The initial exhilaration had passed, leaving him restless. A sense of loss brewed inside him.

Ten years ago, he'd been so full of plans. He'd expected to be retired from the military by now and well on his way to making his fortune. He'd pictured himself with a wife and a house full of children.

Yet here he was at thirty-four years, alone, no wife, and no children. All he could claim as his own was a vendetta for a traitor and an obsession for a woman.

If only Meredith hadn't come to Libby Prison two years ago. If only the prison escape had gone smoothly. If only he could let the war go. If only...

Damn, but he wanted this gnawing in his gut to cease. He wanted things to be as they were—logical, black and white—so that he could move on with his life and stop dreaming about Meredith and wishing for what could never be.

The creak of floorboard squeaked behind him. He didn't turn, because he knew it was Meredith. He knew the sound of her footsteps, her scent.

She moved beside him and stared out at the dewy landscape. The top of her head barely reached his shoulder. The frown lines around her mouth were gone, but her skin was still pale.

He wanted to wrap his arm around her and pull her against him. But he didn't move. "You did a fine job in there today."

She rubbed her forehead. "Thank you. I couldn't have done it without you. You're a natural with children. Do you have any?"

"No." He leaned against the porch rail. "There was a woman once in my life. She wanted babies."

Meredith's shock was undeniable. "You were married?"

"Engaged."

"What happened?"

There'd been a time it had been too painful to think about it. Now it was just a memory. "Isabelle wanted to marry. I wanted to wait until the war ended."

"Why did you wait?"

"Didn't like the idea of leaving a widow or orphan behind."

"And she didn't agree?" He heard the sadness.

"No. She wanted children right away. Married another officer. I heard they've two little ones now and live in Maryland."

"I'm sorry."

Travis turned and stared down at her, amazed at the flurry of feelings he saw in her eyes. She wore her heart on her sleeve.

"Why didn't you tell Nathan we were leaving? He would have helped you if you asked."

"Nathan doesn't need to be worrying about me, not with the new baby." She slid a glance at his profile. "And you said you'd help."

His gaze was sharp. "You trust me."

She raised her chin. "Yes."

"Just like that?" His tone mirrored his doubt.

"Yes."

He frowned. "Don't make me out to be a hero, Meredith. If the evidence points to you, I'll see you in prison."

Chapter Eleven

Rafferty's words may have sounded harsh, but they didn't hold the venom they once had. Now his voice sounded weary, even worried that he would find evidence against her.

"You won't find anything against me. It doesn't exist."

"I hope so, for both our sakes," he said.

The raw honesty in his voice struck a cord of fear. She wasn't afraid of the charges but of her feelings for Rafferty.

Emotions other than just anger ran deep in him and the more she glimpsed the man under the shell, the more her feelings grew.

Maybe if she hadn't seen a different side of him today. Maybe if they hadn't shared a joyous birth together or maybe if they'd not connected, then her heart wouldn't be opening to him. But it was.

To her great misery, she realized she could fall in love with this man.

She needed him to hold her, to tell her everything was going to be fine. But of course, she'd never ask and he'd never offer. So they rode the three miles between the cabins not uttering a word.

When they arrived at Meredith's cottage, they guided their horses into the barn. Rafferty unsaddled the horses and led them into their stalls as Meredith stocked the feed bins with fresh hay and water.

Meredith dug a piece of dried apple out of the feed bucket and fed it the gunman's nag. "There you go, Sam. Did you miss us?"

Rafferty hitched the stall door closed. He paused to stare at her. "That horse can't make the trip," he said quietly.

A wave of protectiveness washed over her. The animals had been her only family these past few months, but deep inside she understood Rafferty was right. She had to let them go.

It was all almost too much to bear. "I know. I'll find a home for her."

He rubbed Blue on the nose. "Better find one for Blue while you're at it."

Her head snapped up. "I'm not leaving him behind. Blue can make the trip."

Sadness deepened the lines of Rafferty's face. "Meredith, he's fine for short hauls into town, but he'll not make it a hundred miles."

She moved to Blue's stall, nudged Rafferty aside and scratched her horse between the ears. "I can't just leave him."

"You'll have to."

Meredith rubbed the horse's velvet-soft nose. "Don't listen to him," she whispered to the horse. "He's just in one of his moods." The horse swished his tail. "I won't leave you."

Frowning, Rafferty tucked his thumbs into his pockets and strolled to his horse's stall. He rechecked the bolt on the stall door. "Meredith, I'm not saying this to be cruel. I don't like being the bad guy. The fact is that a long trip won't be fair to the animal. The trip will kill him."

Meredith chewed her lip. Her mind understood, but her heart ached at the idea of leaving the animal behind. "He's a good animal."

He moved closer. "There'll be someone who'll take him."

She stared into the horse's brown eyes. "He's not as fast as he used to be, but he is sweet-tempered. He'd be a good horse for a child."

"We'll make a point to tell folks that."

This all seemed so unfair. "What about the cats and Shorty?"

He stared at the hound and couldn't seem to hide a warm smile. "There are times when I wonder if the animal has a heartbeat."

She chuckled. "He is a little slow."

"Meredith, he redefines slow."

As if he knew he was being discussed, Shorty, who was napping in the corner, raised his head and yawned, then put his head back down.

Rafferty shook his head. "Only you would take in these animals—or me for that matter."

She sensed Rafferty was trying, but how could he understand how much she cared about her animals? "I didn't go looking for them, they all just kind of found me."

"And it's not in you to turn anyone away."

He pushed himself from the stall and strode toward her. He captured a stray strand of hair that had broken loose from her ribbon.

She didn't turn from the feather-like touch. It felt so good. "It's not as if I've *kept* every animal that ever wandered into my yard. I've had others—once they get stronger some leave or I find homes for them."

"How many animals?"

"What makes you think I'd remember them all?"

"If I had to bet, I'd say you gave a name to each one."

"Maybe a few."

He lifted an eyebrow.

"Okay, I did name them all."

"How many?"

She wanted to lean into him. "Twenty-three—fifteen dogs, seven cats and one raccoon."

"Why do you feel as if you have to save us all, Meredith?" His vivid blue eyes studied every detail of her face.

She moistened her lips. "You needed me."

If he leaned a fraction closer, his lips would be touching hers. A rush of sensations tickled her limbs. She wanted him.

His fingers brushed her cheek. The simple touch brought a blush to Meredith's cheeks and she curled her fingers into a fist as if she'd been burned.

"Meredith." Travis wrapped his strong arms around her shoulders and drew her into his arms and kissed her. Unquestioning, she clung to him. A rich masculine scent enveloped her. She sighed raggedly, letting her worry go. Despite all that lay ahead, she felt wonderfully alive. And not alone.

A small cry caught in her throat as she closed her eyes and leaned into him. He hardly let her catch her breath, his kisses filling her with a desire as hot as the sun.

She drove her hands through his hair, beckoning him. He traced his fingers down the column of her slender neck, kindling her senses. Her thoughts grew incoherent.

His hand slid up her narrow waist and cupped her breast, squeezing gently through the folds of cotton. Her nipples hardened.

She arched her back, pressing her taut breast into his hand. For once she wished she possessed the experience credited to widows.

"Travis, I have to tell you something."

He stilled and raised his head. She could almost see his internal guard rise.

"James and I...we never did this."

He stroked her face. "What are you saying?"

Her mouth was as dry as cotton. "We never made love. He left minutes after our wedding ceremony. He was dead the next time I saw him."

He swallowed. "You are a virgin?"

Heat burned her face. "Yes."

He drew back. "This changes everything."

Tears glistened in her eyes. She laid her hand over his clenched fist. "Please don't let it. I waited the last time and was cheated. Now, I just want this moment.''

''Meredith, it isn't right.'' He sounded as if pain ravaged his body.

Driven by instinct, she slid her hand over his flat belly to his belt buckle. The need to feel him overrode fear. Her fingertips slid beyond the belt to his hardness.

He sucked in his breath, then captured her hand and drew her fingers away from his hardness to his lips. ''I should back away, but I want you too much to care,'' he ground out.

''Good.''

He nibbled the tips of each finger. She sucked in a breath.

He tugged her forward and threaded his hands into her tangled curls. He drove her lips open with his tongue and plunged into the velvet softness of her mouth. A low guttural moan escaped his lips. His rigid body radiated pent-up energy.

Tantalized by longing, she matched the thrusts of his tongue with her own. The control she had always prided herself on shattered.

It felt so good simply to feel.

''You won't be sorry?''

''No.''

Travis guided her to a pile of fresh hay. He

shrugged off his coat and covered the prickly hay. Then he pulled off his shirt. The bandage accentuated the deep bronze of his muscled chest. His skin glistened in the moonlight.

He pulled her down and coaxed her body back against the straw, then draped his long, lean body over hers. The hay prickled her skin.

"You deserve a real bed," he growled. He nestled his thigh between her legs.

"It doesn't matter."

"It does." He kissed the column of her long neck.

His bearded chin rubbed her tender skin, sending shivers down her spine. She felt shameless and wanton but didn't care. She shivered as a pleasant ache throbbed between her legs.

Travis let his gaze slide over Meredith like a lazy caress. "I've wanted this since the moment I first saw you years ago," he said.

Sweat glistened on his forehead in the moonlight. His black hair hung recklessly in his eyes. Her breath quickened.

His gaze dropped to the rapid rise and fall of her breasts. He reached for the tiny pearl buttons that trailed between her breasts and slowly unfastened each one. He pushed back the folds of her bodice. When she tried to cover herself, he pulled her hands away, trapping them above her head. "Let me look at you," he rasped.

Only her gauzy chemise covered the hard peaks of her breasts. She could barely breathe. He lowered his head and suckled her through the fabric, then nipped at her soft skin with his even, white teeth.

She moaned, squirming under him. Passion coursed through her body. She wanted him so badly that holding back hurt.

He released her hand to slide his own hand up the inside of her skirt. He gripped the top of her pantaloons and, when they didn't give way, he pulled until they tore. She raised her hips so he could slide the remnants over her silken legs.

He lifted the fabric of her skirt up to her waist. Primitive desire glimmered in his eyes as he stared at her. "You are beautiful," he whispered.

His long, callused fingers found her center and began to stroke. The wild passion he stirred in her touched every nerve in her body. Helpless, she closed her eyes and savored the expert touch. "What are you doing to me?"

He chuckled. "Loving you."

Suddenly he moved away from her, leaving her skin cold. She opened her eyes to see him strip off his boots and pants.

Panic flickered when she caught sight of his arousal. Perhaps, this wasn't such a good idea after all.

But before she could voice the first doubt, he was back on top of her, straddling her, pressing her into the hay with his weight.

He covered her body with his kisses, kissed her again and chased away her worries. He fired her up inside.

She hesitated, then almost coyly smoothed her hand over his buttocks and along his thigh. She heard his breath hiss through his teeth, saw the muscles strain in his neck.

Her hands shook as she reached the tangle of curls near his center. The thought of touching him consumed her.

He groaned when her fingertips brushed his hardness. Uncertain but determined, she slid her hand down to the tip and circled it with her thumb.

He captured her hand, kissed it. "Not yet," he growled, his eyes sparking with dark passion.

She moistened her lips. "Did I do something wrong?"

"No, darlin'. I don't want this over before it starts."

He straddled her and she instinctively stroked

the outside of his thighs and he looked as if he teetered on the brink of madness as he stared down at her.

He cupped her face in his hands. "There is only us, here, right now," he said fiercely. He kissed her hard on the lips as if branding her.

"The two of us," she whispered. "Now."

Travis touched her at her intimate juncture, now wet and swollen with desire. She gasped. He teased her velvety folds with his thumb, and she arched against him and moaned.

Pressure built inside her as she staggered close to the abyss.

"Please." Her voice was husky, full of emotion. How did she make him understand what she wanted him to do?

"Soon," he breathed against her ear. "This is too good to rush."

He took her hand and pressed it against his manhood, straining against her naked thigh. Her skin burned with passion as her fingers cupped him.

He suckled the rosy tip of her breast then trailed kisses down her smooth, flat stomach.

This was more than she'd ever dreamed of. "I don't want to wait."

"I want to make this last, but I want you," he said.

"No more waiting ever again," she whispered, her voice husky. She opened her legs.

The muscles and veins in his neck pulsed and his jaw tensed with unleashed passion as he thrust into Meredith. She clutched his shoulders and sucked in a breath, overwhelmed by the sensations of pleasure and pain as he ripped through the barrier.

Travis stilled as she adjusted to him. "I'm not sorry I'm the first."

As pain turned to pleasure, she started to move her hips. "Nor am I."

His intoxicating scent engulfed her senses. She stroked her fingertips over his bare buttocks, then cupped the hard flesh.

Need strained his sinewy muscles. She pushed her hips upward, beckoning him. He buried his face against the soft skin of her neck and the tangle of her coppery curls. His breathing was hard, urgent.

Travis kissed her face then trailed tiny kisses along the column of her throat until she arched her back. His thrusts grew harder, more insistent.

She bucked when he slid his fingers to her soft

juncture. She moaned his name. He was driving her insane.

Matching his rhythm, she moved to the timeless dance, letting her instinct take over. She wrapped her slender legs around his waist.

She savored the feel of his weight crushing against her breasts, his coarse chest hair teasing her skin, and the slick, salty sweat coating their bodies.

He withdrew and entered her now as if half out of his mind with fever. She moaned and took in all of him, praying this moment would never end even as she begged for release.

Travis slowed his pace so he could watch her tumble into the sweet madness. When she thought she could bear no more, the storm reached its tempest. She screamed his name, dug her nails into his back and held on to him, fearing she'd lose her mind.

Travis ground his teeth, his face grim, and pushed deep inside her. Every muscle in his body constricted. He closed his eyes, called her name in agony, and then joined her in a perfect, mindless moment as he spilled his seed inside her.

He collapsed against Meredith, his heart thundering against her skin as if he'd run a dozen miles.

Meredith's head fell back against the hay. Minutes passed as they lay together, sweaty and fully spent. Their hearts hammered in unison and she savored the delicious warmth.

He spooned his body against hers, holding her tight.

Meredith had never felt so relaxed, so complete. She understood that tomorrow they'd leave.

And that everything would change.

A fanciful idea struck her and, before she thought to censure it, she said, "I wish we could run away. For once in my life I want to just forget obligations and consequences."

Rafferty drew her closer to his hard chest. "Actions always have consequences, Meredith."

Chapter Twelve

They made love again. This time Travis took his time with Meredith, savoring every inch of her soft body. When they were satiated, they slept together in the hay until morning.

With the night gone, reality beckoned like the bright sun. There was no denying that the time had come to leave.

Silent, they rose and dressed. Neither spoke as Travis guided Meredith back to the house. He reached for the doorknob, twisted it and shoved it wide open. Sunlight streamed into Meredith's cabin.

For an instant, the scene didn't register in Meredith's mind.

It did in Travis's. "Damn it."

As his warrior's eyes canvassed the room, Meredith stared in shocked horror at the overturned chairs, the broken crocks of sugar and flour littering the floor, the blankets strewn and slashed and the overturned tables.

It looked as if a windstorm had swept through the room.

Meredith pressed her fingertips to her mouth. The violation she felt sickened her. Someone had been in her home and had destroyed her belongings. "I've never had this kind of trouble before. Who could have done this?"

Travis righted an overturned chair. "They're looking for something."

She looked over her shoulder at a torn curtain. "What?"

He raised his gun and started to move toward her room. "I don't know. And until I'm sure they're gone, stay put."

Goose bumps puckered her flesh as Travis moved away from her and began to search the cabin. From the main room, she could see her mattress had been turned over, sliced down the middle and her blankets lay in a tattered pile in the corner.

Travis looked under her bed and then moved through the kitchen. Satisfied, they were alone, he released the hammer of his gun. "Whoever did this is gone."

She went into the bedroom. Her clothes lay in a heap on the floor and on top of them lay her wedding photograph. The frame was twisted, the glass broken.

Gingerly she shook the broken shards of glass from the frame. The once-smooth photo was now scarred and scratched. "Who could have done this?"

Rafferty moved behind her, studied the picture over her shoulder. "I don't know." He took the picture. "You look different there. Younger. Happier."

She studied her bright smile. "Aren't all brides?"

He looked at the picture again. "James was just a kid."

"Twenty-one."

"He looked like he hadn't started shaving."

She smiled. "We felt so grown-up, so smart that day, yet we were just babies. It's as if we were playing dress-up. Me in my fairy-tale gown, he in his freshly pressed uniform."

"The wedding was a big fancy affair, no doubt," he said, frowning.

"Yes. James's mother invited the whole town.

The day before we wed, he received his orders. He knew he was going to leave with his men right after the ceremony the next day, but he didn't tell me. He wanted the day to be perfect.''

A lingering guilt washed over her as she looked at James. She realized that if she'd met him today, she'd not have married him. Whatever love they'd shared was gone.

So much of life had changed, been lost, since that day.

The trespassers had bent the frame. Suddenly she needed to right it. She struggled with the twisted silver, but the frame wouldn't budge.

"Let me." Travis took the frame and with his strong hands tried to bend it back. "We'll have the blacksmith in town look at it."

"It doesn't really matter. It's part of a life that's gone forever."

He studied her face and shook his head. "No. We'll fix it. Some things shouldn't be forgotten."

Rafferty laid his hands on her shoulders. "Whoever did this will come back," he said. "We need to get into town."

She laid her hand over his fingers. "I thought we weren't going into town."

"It's safer for you in town right now. Once we

figure out who's behind this, then we'll leave. Pack what you need.''

She found her carpetbag strewn in a corner and began the tedious task of picking through the heap of her clothes. ''Almost everything is destroyed. There's so little to save.''

''Do the best you can. We'll buy what you need in town.''

''Maybe all this was random—a very unfortunate coincidence.''

''It wasn't.'' He glanced out the bedroom window. Grasslands skimmed blue sky. But there wasn't a soul in sight. ''They'll be back.''

She shoved her brush, comb and silver-trimmed hand mirror into the bag. ''How can you be so sure?''

He nodded to the picture frame. ''They'd have taken that for one. It's silver. Your money box was not disturbed. The food in the kitchen's untouched. No, whoever was here was looking for something specific.''

''I don't have anything of real value,'' she whispered.

''Maybe they just wanted you.'' He frowned at the mess.

A shiver snaked down her body as she put the

last of her belongings into the bag. "I just don't understand this."

"Neither do I, but now's not the time or place to question. We're leaving."

Ten minutes later her bag was packed. Rafferty had saddled his horse and Blue. He took her bag.

As he laced her bag to his pommel, she studied his face. He was frowning, but the expression no longer intimidated her. Already she'd come to recognize the look. He was angry yes, but not at her. He was worried and trying to think through all the possible scenarios so he could head off trouble.

Her heart tightened as she watched him. There was so much to love about that man. So much.

"Meredith, are you listening?"

Startled, she blinked. "What?"

"Get the saddle blankets."

"Sure. And I'll get the other animals, too."

He swung his head around. "The what?"

"The other animals. Sam, the cats, Shorty."

"Excuse me?"

Her protective instincts went into high gear. "They have to come. It's not safe for them here. Whoever destroyed my house could return."

"Absolutely not."

212   *Rafferty's Bride*

She folded her arms over her chest. "They don't go, I don't go."

Travis shoved his fingers through his hair. "If I weren't in such a rush, I'd argue."

She smiled. "But you won't."

He muttered an oath. "Pack them up."

She grinned and handed him a kitten with black paws and a white face. "I'll get the other kittens."

The kitten licked his face. "Terrific."

Ten minutes later, they were on the trail. Travis stole a glance at Meredith as they rode into town. She held on to a lead line attached to the nag's bridle as the animal clumped happily behind her. Attached to the nag's back was a basket filled with the mother cat and kittens. Shorty, the hound, trailed behind barking at stray rabbits.

When had he changed from a respected soldier feared by men to leader of a damn circus procession?

And when had he lost control?

Worse, why didn't he care?

When he was with Meredith everything just felt right. And it went beyond the physical attraction. He wasn't fool enough to think it was anything close to love.

Love.

Lord, help him.

He couldn't be in love with Meredith Carter.

He still wanted her in his bed. Once had not been enough. No, never enough.

But love? He'd been in love before with Isabelle and that had been a heady, out-of-control feeling that left as quickly as it came. What he felt for Meredith was completely different. Deeper, stronger.

Hell, he hadn't yet figured out what had happened at Libby Prison. Yet, he was waxing on about love.

He let out a sigh. He was certain now that whatever had happened that fateful night, Meredith Carter hadn't acted out of spite or anger. Maybe she'd slipped up and, without even realizing it, mentioned a critical detail to the wrong person. She'd had a lot on her plate that night. And she was tired. No doubt, alone and afraid.

The image bothered him and he forced it aside. If he had his way, she'd not struggle like that ever again.

He owed Meredith, could admit he cared about her, but whatever he was feeling, it sure as hell wasn't love.

* * *

It took less than a half hour to reach Trail's End. The farming town was small, sporting only a single main street and a collection of weathered buildings. The saloon and the mercantile were the largest buildings, each two stories with wide front windows. The other buildings were little more than dugouts with false fronts.

Travis chose the eastern trail into town because, last week when he'd been in town, he'd noted folks seemed to congregate on the west side. He'd hoped to slip into town and stall the onslaught of questions he knew would come before he had a chance to meet with the sheriff.

But the trail into town was anything except quiet. Hundreds of people, wagons and horses that weren't there last week filled the streets. "What the devil?"

"The new doctor," Meredith supplied. "He's due in town today. People have come to see him."

Travis shoved a hand through his hair. "Of course. My timing's been off since I left Washington."

"Maybe no one will notice us."

"With this procession. Don't count on it."

"Miss Meredith!" A young boy who looked to be about ten bolted out the church's back door.

Travis shifted in his saddle. "Perfect."

"Miss Meredith!" The boy's brown pants were stained with grass at the knees and his white shirt was splattered with mud. The child pushed back a lock of blond hair. "Mrs. Harper is gonna be glad to see you. I think she was fixing to send the sheriff out to your place if you didn't show up today."

Meredith's smile was warm, genuine, as she pulled her horse to a stop in front of the weathered church. "That's sweet of her to worry. But as you can see I am just fine, Danny."

The boy's gap-toothed grin vanished when he glared at Travis. "Who's he?"

Travis shifted, ready to reply, but Meredith answered first. "Captain Travis Rafferty, meet Danny White."

The boy shoved his hands in his pockets. "He looks mean."

Travis tipped his hat back with his forefinger. "I am mean."

Meredith glared at Travis. "Danny, don't you believe a word he says. He's not mean at all. He saved my life."

Something in her tone touched the deepest part of Travis's soul. He pictured her at his side for a lifetime. For a moment, he struggled to breathe properly.

Meredith tugged the lead line forward. "Danny, would you take this horse over to the livery and ask Rob to look after him? I'll be by soon and have a word with him about his care and feeding."

Distracted, the boy tore his gaze from Travis and settled it on the horse. He took the rope as he studied the horse. "He's just an old nag."

Meredith lifted her chin. "He's a fine animal, just in need of good care. Make sure you tell Rob he likes oats. And mind you're careful with the basket. There are kittens inside."

"Kittens!" Danny stood on tiptoe and peered into the basket. The three kittens had awoken. They'd started to mew and reached for the lip of the basket. "You think I could have one?"

Meredith laughed. "Talk to your ma."

"They got names?" Danny asked.

Meredith leaned over and pushed the black-and-white one back into the basket. "That one's Sparky. Always gets into trouble. The tabby that's kinda quiet is Spot and the one chasing its tail is Spooky."

The boy glanced up at Meredith, his blue eyes

sparkling with excitement. "Maybe Ma will let me keep them all."

Meredith lifted an eyebrow. "Maybe. But just in case she doesn't, tell anyone you see that the kittens and all my animals need a home."

The boy squinted his left eye and tilted his head to the right. "What for? Don't you want them no more?"

Meredith's hands trembled a little as she tightened her reins around her hand. "I want them all, but I may be going away for a while."

The boy squinted against the sun as he stared at her. "Where you going?"

"East."

"Where East?"

Meredith stiffened, and her smile became forced. "Washington."

"That's mighty far! How come you're going so far?"

Travis leaned forward in his saddle. "Boy, just do as Mrs. Carter asked. Now hurry along."

Travis's deep voice left no room for argument. The boy scampered toward the livery with the horse in tow. "Come on, Shorty, I bet Ma's got a bone for you." Shorty barked and followed behind the child, wagging his tail.

Travis stared at Meredith's profile. The sparkle

had gone out of her eyes. He didn't like seeing her so sad. "They'll find homes."

The smile she offered didn't touch her eyes. "I know."

He moved his horse beside hers and his leg grazed hers. "You'll get more animals one day."

"I know." Her voice sounded stilted, as if it were all she could do not to cry.

He supposed he could have kept throwing nice words at her, but the plain truth was that none were likely to do any good now. She was losing what she cared about and it hurt.

He understood.

He'd lived through the same feelings often enough. Words just didn't matter when your insides were in knots.

"There's a small restaurant in town. I saw it when I first came."

"Jackson's Café."

"That's it. Any good?"

She sniffed. "The steaks are good."

"Just what I need." She looked as if she could use a good meal, one she didn't have to serve.

Meredith brushed a tear from her face before she met his gaze. "I thought we were going to see the sheriff?"

As he stared at her watery gaze, he wasn't interested in much more than sitting and having a normal meal with her. They'd been through a lot together. Hell, they'd made love. But he'd never done anything nice for her. And she deserved something nice.

But she was right. He wanted to see the sheriff before they ate. Her safety came first.

He squeezed her hand. ''Once we see the sheriff, we'll eat.''

A sigh shuddered from her chest and a bit of color returned to her cheeks. ''I'd like that.''

As they rode down the dusty main street together, Travis was aware that everyone had stopped what they were doing to watch them. Women gathered in clusters, menfolk set aside their chores and the children stopped playing as they passed.

Folks just naturally smiled when they saw Meredith. Many of the women waved and called out to her. She knew all the children by name and they swarmed around her.

But as soon as anyone's gaze shifted from her to him, the smile turned to a scowl.

Without a word spoken, Travis knew he wasn't welcome in Trail's End.

A rush of shame washed over him. He was taking her away from her friends, the only home she'd known.

He steeled himself against the unwanted thoughts.

He'd come to Trail's End to do a job and he owed it to his men who'd been killed in the escape attempt to see it through.

Once he found out who was after Meredith, they'd head east. Back there they'd figure out who was behind this and then he'd be his old self.

Travis glanced over at Meredith. So lovely. He remembered how soft her mouth had felt against his. How her body had felt under him.

Hell, who was he kidding?

He'd never be his old self.

Chapter Thirteen

The sheriff's office was at the north end of town. Sunlight slanted across the adobe-style building's rough gray walls and reflected on the murky water in the horse trough out front. A bay tied to the hitching post nickered as Meredith and Travis dismounted.

Travis tied the horse reins to the post then guided Meredith by the elbow into the jail. She climbed the steps, paused on the boardwalk and then faced him, eye to eye. "Do you think what's happening here is connected to the past?"

His gaze was intense. "It has to be. Those men who shot me were only interested in killing you."

She paled. "Why, after all this time?"

He took her hand in his. "I don't know. The pieces don't fit yet, but they will, given time." He traced circles on her palm with his thumb. "Do you trust me?"

She nodded without hesitating. "I do."

Though she'd been by the building a hundred times, this was the first time she'd ever been inside. "For criminals and ruffians," Sheriff Harper had said. "No ladies allowed."

There wasn't a soul in the main area or the two barred cells. Morning sun trickled into the dim room by way of a barred window. The only furniture in the spartan room were the single cots in each cell, a scarred desk, a chair near the door and a gun rack sporting three rifles chained together.

The simple room was a true reflection of Sheriff Harper's no-nonsense style. The clean floors, fresh sheets on the cots and the scent of beeswax were Mrs. Harper's doing.

Travis tugged Meredith behind him. "Hello!"

"The sheriff usually goes home for breakfast this time of day," Meredith offered.

"And leaves the place wide open?" Travis didn't hide the disgust in his voice.

"Trail's End is a quiet place," she explained. "Except for a drunken cowhand or two during the drives, we have little trouble."

The answer didn't seem to satisfy Travis, a man

who'd lived his life on alert, his guard always up. "Anybody here?"

"Hold your horses," a man shouted just outside the door. There was no mistaking the Georgia accent.

"That's the sheriff," Meredith said.

Travis faced the door, tucking Meredith beside him. "About time."

Sheriff Harper, dressed in denim pants, a white shirt and vest with a dented tin star pinned to the lapel, strolled through the door. The sheriff's arms were thick and his wire-rim spectacles were taped together on the left side. He was carrying a tray of food covered with a red-checkered cloth.

Immediately he set the tray down and his hand slid to his gun. "Can I help you?"

Travis turned. He took in the gray hair, wrinkles and bright clear eyes. "Sheriff Harper?"

"My wife was talking about a stranger last week and, by her description, I'd say she was talking about you." Suspicion laced each word.

Travis nodded. "That's right."

Meredith stepped out from behind Travis. "Sheriff Harper."

The old man's gaze shifted to Meredith and his face split into a wide grin. "Well, it's about time you came to town, Miss Meredith. Edith was getting worried and ready to send a posse for you."

Meredith moved away from Travis and accepted his bear hug easily. "I've had my hands full with patients, Sheriff. How's that tooth of yours doing?"

He bit down a couple of times, testing. "Better. I been drinking that god-awful medicine just like you said. It tastes like hell but it works."

She laughed. "Good."

Pleasantries aside, the lawman pinned his attention on Travis. "Who's he?"

Meredith shifted back to Travis. "I'd like you to meet Captain Travis Rafferty."

Sheriff Harper's face showed no sign of welcome. "And what brings a *Yank* captain to town?"

Travis didn't shrink from the old man. "I came to Trail's End to arrest Meredith."

His gnarled hands slid to his gun. "You ain't taking Meredith anywhere."

Travis braced. "We'll talk about that later. Right now we've got more pressing business."

"Ain't nothing more pressing, boy, than talking about you arresting Meredith."

Meredith stepped between the men. "Sheriff, Travis saved my life. He was shot at the homestead last week, fending off two gunmen who wanted to kill me.''

The old man's demeanor turned menacing. ''At your homestead? Who were these men?''

''She doesn't know,'' Travis said, taking control of the conversation. ''I was hoping you might tell me. They would have passed through town last week.''

The older man shoved his hand through his gray mane. ''The only stranger in town last week was you, Captain.''

''Has there been anyone since last week?'' Travis persisted. ''Someone ransacked Meredith's place last night.''

Muttering an oath, the sheriff hooked his thumbs in his gun belt. ''No one's been through town. Meredith's never had trouble before. Why now? What kind of trouble has followed you west, Captain?''

Before Travis would form another question, Mrs. Harper burst into the jailhouse. Breathless, she still wore her kitchen apron, which stretched tight over her round stomach and was covered with flour. ''Meredith Carter, why are you giving your animals away? I just passed Danny White by the mercantile pleading with his ma to let him keep your kittens.''

"Mrs. Harper," Meredith said, smiling easily. "I'm leaving town."

"What are you talking about? You can't leave." Mrs. Harper's face soured as if she'd bit into a lemon. She swung around and faced Travis. "You're the one!"

Travis's surprise was evident. "Ma'am?"

"The one who was lingering around town last week. I told you about him, Fox, but you were too sick to listen."

Sheriff Harper shifted his stance. "I'm all ears now, Edith."

His wife lifted her chin, clearly happy to supply details. "He was real clever all right, but there was no denying he was up to something."

The sheriff lifted a brow. "When was he in town?"

"Thursday before last," Travis supplied.

Mrs. Harper stopped to think. "That's right. I was taking my mending to Martha's, so it was laundry day. Yes, it was Thursday. The very same day Meredith tended your tooth."

"I was laid up most of last week. That stuff you gave me made sleepy as all get-out," the Sheriff explained. "Edith, you notice anyone else?"

"Well, we got a few men. There were two of

them. They stayed just long enough to water their horses and grab supplies.''

"Did you notice which way they were headed?'' Travis asked.

"West.''

Travis nodded. "Toward Meredith's.''

"One had a terrible scar,'' Mrs. Harper said.

Meredith inched closer to Travis. "One of the men who shot the captain had a terrible scar. I buried him myself.''

The sheriff's anger made his fingers twitch over his pistol. "I never did like you out there by yourself.''

"Did you notice anything else?'' Travis said. The precious few details weren't getting them any closer to the truth.

Mrs. Harper held up a finger. "As a matter of fact, I saw him lingering around the telegraph office. Maybe he sent a telegram. I meant to double back and ask about the telegram, but I was so busy with Fox, I forgot.''

Travis took Meredith by the elbow. "I'll check it out.''

The sheriff blocked the exit with his body. "Not so fast. I want details and I mean all of them.''

Travis tensed. Meredith suspected he was a

man who worked alone, had never been account-able to anyone. Still, Travis told his story of Libby Prison, meeting Meredith, the breakout and his reasons for coming. The lines in the sheriff's face grew deeper with each passing minute.

Mrs. Harper's jaw clenched with anger. ''I don't like this one bit. Not one bit.''

For several anxious seconds, Travis and the Harpers squared off, their eyes alive with anger.

''You aren't going anywhere with this stranger,'' Mrs. Harper said. ''I just won't allow it.''

Travis clearly didn't agree with the woman, but out of respect for her age, he held back his opin-ion.

''I want to go back,'' Meredith said, hoping to ?head off trouble. The Harpers looked at her as if she'd gone daft. ''It's time to bury the past once and for all.''

''Honey, you can't go back,'' Mrs. Harper ex-claimed. ''You won't get a fair trial.''

She took the old woman's hand in hers. ''Go-ing back isn't about the trial for me anymore. I know I am innocent of the charges.''

Mrs. Harper squeezed her hand. ''Meredith, in-nocent people end up in jail, especially when they're dealing with a stacked deck of cards.''

Travis's voice was low, dangerous. "If this even comes to trial, I will guarantee that Meredith gets a fair one."

Sheriff Harper studied Travis's face for a long moment. "I think you believe that, Captain. But the truth is, once you get to Washington, events will be out of your control. There's no telling what will happen. We can't protect Meredith when she's two thousand miles away."

"She has to go," Travis said.

"She isn't going anywhere," the sheriff repeated.

"Sheriff," Meredith said steadily. "It's time for me to visit my late husband's grave and let go of him once and for all."

The lines around Mrs. Harper's eyes deepened. "Your James is gone, Meredith. Seeing his grave won't do him a bit of good."

"But it will help his mother, Mrs. Carter. She and I need to forgive each other and let go of the pain. And I need to forgive myself for surviving when so many I loved didn't."

Tears glistened in Mrs. Harper's eyes. "You're too hard on yourself, Meredith. You didn't do anything wrong."

Meredith lifted her chin. "I can't build a new life until I let go of the past. And for the first time in a long time, I want to let go. I want to marry again and have children.''

Mrs. Harper shook her head sadly. ''You don't need to go back. George Walker will marry you tomorrow and give you all you're asking for.''

Travis stiffened but said nothing.

Meredith smoothed her hands over her skirt. ''I've got to set things right and I trust Travis to help me through this, Mrs. Harper.''

The old woman's watery eyes sharpened. ''What did you say?''

She smiled. ''I said I trust him.''

''No you said *Travis.* Fox did you hear her say *Travis?*''

The sheriff sighed. ''I sure did. She's been calling him *Travis* since she arrived.''

Confused, Meredith looked to Travis. His expression was cloaked, but his eyes were keen.

''And she *trusts* him,'' Mrs. Harper said. ''Known him less than a week and she *trusts* him. The minute I laid eyes on him, I knew we had trouble.''

Meredith pressed her fingertips to her right temple. A headache was starting to brew. ''Why does it matter what I call *Captain Rafferty.*''

Mrs. Harper eyed Travis as if she were sizing him up in a way she hadn't before. ''Dear, a woman doesn't call a man by his given name unless there's something going on between them."

Meredith quickly glanced at Travis. Guilt washed over her and she felt her cheeks warm. Travis had made no promises and she'd not pretend it was any more than it was, even if she loved him. Once this was settled, Travis would move on through life without her. "There's nothing going on between *Captain Rafferty* and me."

Travis watched her with a keen interest.

"How many days was you two alone?" Sheriff Harper snorted.

Meredith didn't like the sheriff's tone. "Ten. What's that have to do with anything?"

"Lord Almighty," Mrs. Harper wailed, a bit too dramatically. "And I'll bet you saw him in his wherewithal."

Meredith felt as if she'd been swept into a maelstrom. "He was my patient. And he was unconscious."

The sheriff coughed. "He's looking fit to me, and my guess is he's been up and about for days."

Groaning, Meredith glanced at Travis. "Would you help me out?"

Something had shifted in him as if he'd come to a decision. "What do you want me to say?"

Very aware that everyone was watching her, Meredith forced her fisted fingers to relax. "Tell them that nothing significant happened between us."

Travis rubbed his jaw studying her. "I can't say that."

Meredith groaned. "Yes, you can."

The sheriff patted his thumb on the pearl handle of his pistol. "Me and Edith are the closest Meredith has to kin. And kin looks after kin."

Meredith's eyes widened. "I don't need looking after."

Ignoring her, the sheriff looked to his wife. "Get the minister."

Mrs. Harper nodded gravely. "I'll have him back here in two shakes. They'll be married by lunch."

"No!" Meredith shouted. "Mrs. Harper, don't you move an inch."

The older woman lingered, not quite sure what to do.

Travis laid his hand on Meredith's shoulders. His fingers sent a bolt of energy through her body. "Someone should look after you."

The touch felt too intimate. She took a step forward to break the connection. "Is this your idea of help?"

"You said you wanted me to say something."

"You're making me sound like a weakling who needs looking after."

He shook his head. "I didn't say you were weak. I admire your strength."

The tenderness in his voice was nearly her undoing. She had kept her newfound love for Travis tightly bottled. And would continue to do so as long as he kept matters light. She'd have preferred a burst of Rafferty's temper over the tenderness in his eyes, which threatened to shatter her resolve.

Meredith kept her voice even, controlled, despite the fact that she wanted to scream. "I want you to tell the Harpers that nothing happened, so that we can get our supplies and leave for Washington. I don't want any more talk of marriage."

Travis knew he stood at a crossroads. The Harpers were no match for him. He'd outfoxed the enemy for too many years not to find a way out of this corner.

But the truth was, he didn't want to escape. He wanted Meredith. And the idea of her returning to Trail's End after the trial and marrying George Walker didn't sit well with him at all.

Sheriff Harper lifted a bushy eyebrow. "Captain, what exactly went on out there during those ten days and nine *nights?*''

He understood the direction of Harper's mind. ''I'll marry her.''

''Thank the Lord,'' Mrs. Harper wailed.

Meredith wanted to bolt. ''Well, I'm not marrying him.''

Travis lifted an eyebrow. In a voice as smooth as silk, he said, ''Meredith, we have to set things right.''

''That does it!'' the sheriff said. ''You're marrying him.''

''I'll get the reverend,'' Mrs. Harper said, scurrying out the door before Meredith could protest.

Color burned Meredith's cheeks. ''I am not marrying this man.''

The sheriff lifted an eyebrow. ''Too late to say no, Meredith. Time to fix what's wrong.''

''Nothing is wrong!'' she wailed. Her back was as rigid as a bowstring. ''Captain Rafferty is going to help me clear my name. That is all.''

Travis was careful not to touch her, for fear she'd bolt. ''Like it or not, Meredith, everything has changed between us since I arrived.''

Meredith's face paled. ''Nothing has changed,'' she lied. Her eyes were wide, full of unspoken emotion that both scared and comforted him. "I don't think you even like me."

"I like you just fine." His voice was rough. Lord, he wanted her, and not just for a handful of nights but forever.

Travis took Meredith's hands in his. "Marry me, Meredith."

"Why?" She looked more frightened than he'd ever seen her.

"I don't know. Marriage between us doesn't make sense. I do know that if you're married to me, I'll be able to protect you better when we get to Washington." He refused to lie.

"Protection," she whispered. She studied his face for a long moment. "This is about protection?"

"Partly."

"This is insane."

"No argument here," Travis said.

The sheriff straightened. "So what's it gonna be, Rafferty? You gonna do right by Meredith?"

"I'm more than willing. The rest is up to her," Travis said.

"Meredith?" the sheriff said.

She swallowed. "Yes."

Chapter Fourteen

Fifteen minutes later, the minister rushed into the jailhouse. Reverend Poindexter was a young man, not more than thirty. He wore an apron dusted with flour over his black pants and a white shirt with shirtsleeves rolled up past his elbows. His thick black air looked windswept, as if he'd run all the way from the picnic to the jailhouse. "Fox, what's wrong? Edith said it was an emergency."

Sheriff Harper rose from his chair positioned behind his desk. "Not exactly an emergency, but we need a marriage ceremony."

Reverend Poindexter blinked. "A marriage ceremony? Can't it wait? I'm right in the middle of frying hush puppies at the picnic."

The sheriff motioned Travis and Meredith forward. "Can't wait and it won't take but a minute."

Reverend Poindexter looked at Meredith, Travis and then at Meredith again. "Mrs. Carter, how you doing today?"

She pulled in a breath. "I'm fine."

"Who's getting married?" the young minister asked.

"Me," Meredith said.

"Well, I figured this was coming, but George Walker didn't say a word. Where is George anyway?"

"Mrs. Carter is marrying me," Travis said impatiently.

The minister's shock was clear. "Who are you?"

"Travis Rafferty," he said.

Mrs. Harper huffed through the front door, pulling a lace handkerchief from her pocket. She fanned her red face. "Are they hitched yet?"

"No," the sheriff said. "We just got through with introductions."

Clearly confused, the minister asked, "Can someone explain what's going on?"

"Long story," Mrs. Harper said. "We'll tell you all about it at the picnic. But I want these two hitched before anyone changes their mind."

"Normally, I like to visit with the happy couple before the nuptials," the minister said.

"No time for that," said the sheriff.

The minister hesitated. "Well...if everyone's sure."

"I'm not changing my mind," Travis said in a loud, clear voice.

Meredith glanced at Travis. She looked scared, ready to run. "Me neither."

Reverend Poindexter shrugged off his surprise. "Mrs. Carter, this is sudden. It's the last thing I ever would have expected."

She nodded. "I know."

"George know about this?"

She fidgeted with her cuff. "No. I'm going to have to have a talk with him."

He studied her a moment longer then untied his apron and set it aside. He unrolled his shirtsleeves and pulled a small Bible from his breast pocket. "All right then."

Travis moved next to Meredith and took her hand in his. Her fingers were cold, but her grip was strong.

"Dearly beloved," the minister began.

"Wait!" Meredith pulled her hand from Travis's. She tugged off her wedding band and tucked it into her pocket. "Sorry, you can start again."

Travis's heart, which had stopped for one agonizing second, started beating again.

The ceremony wasn't fancy by anyone's standards. The trappings and such that went with a wedding meant nothing to him, but women liked that kind of thing and he wanted to make Meredith happy. She deserved the very best.

Her face was a mask of cool reserve as she recited her vows. He'd have given a year's pay to know what was going on in her head.

The vows were exchanged quickly and efficiently.

"Well, I suppose you can kiss her now," Reverend Poindexter said. Sheriff Harper's shoulders relaxed and his hand eased away from his gun. Mrs. Harper cried.

Travis wanted to kiss her, to spirit her away to a hotel room, shut the world out and have her all to himself. But with an audience, he settled for a gentle squeeze of her hand.

She looked up at him and managed an uneasy smile.

He wanted to give her the world. "When we get to Washington, I'll buy you a ring."

"My old one is fine." She dug it out of her pocket.

Like hell it was. "I'll buy you a new one."

She didn't argue and her eyes seemed to brighten. "Fresh starts all around."

"Exactly."

Reverend Poindexter reached for his apron. "I'll see you all then at the picnic. I've got hot oil in the kettle and a half-dozen young boys circling around and ready to deep-fry rocks and sticks." He started to the doorway then paused. "Good luck to you both."

After he disappeared, Mrs. Harper beamed as she dabbed the corner of her eye. "This is a wonderful day for a wedding. The doctor's welcome picnic is underway and it's the perfect time to introduce the captain to everyone."

"That sounds lovely," Meredith said.

The sheriff grinned like the Cheshire cat. "I reckon a stop by the picnic would be good." Steel threaded his voice. Travis would have declined if Meredith hadn't looked so relieved.

His bride needed time to absorb the sudden shift in their lives. And tomorrow, he'd be taking her away from Trail's End and there was no telling when they'd be back. "Lead the way, Sheriff."

Sheriff Harper clearly relaxed when he realized Travis wasn't going to argue.

As they made their way down the boardwalk

past Closed signs that dangled in the store windows, Mrs. Harper chatted nosily to Meredith about a half-dozen other weddings she'd attended in the past year.

Travis stole a glance at Meredith, who'd barely spoken since the ceremony. As comfort, he took her hand in his. The simple touch made her jump and she looked up at him anxiously.

"You all right?" he asked.

Her hands were ice-cold. "Of course."

"It'll be fine."

Mrs. Harper was unaware of the emotions storming between them. "Except for the Fourth of July and Christmas, the town rarely comes together like this. But a new doctor is reason to celebrate. Everyone's gone all out. Of course, the doctor ain't shown up yet. But," she said managing a bright smile, "I'm not going to fret over that. He'll be here. And this is a joyous day."

"Everything's going to be fine," Meredith said.

Edith Harper's eyes welled up again. "Aren't you sweet, trying to make me feel better when you've just married a near stranger."

Meredith paled and quickly glanced up at Travis as if the weight of Mrs. Harper's words had struck home.

With nothing else to say, the four walked to the picnic in silence. Just as Mrs. Harper had promised, everyone had gathered at the edge of town.

A long table, made of wood and sawhorses, was filled with an array of pies, cakes, breads and meats. On a makeshift stage, a trio of men had struck up a lively tune with their fiddles. Children ran around, giggling. Young girls gathered in clusters, exchanging smiles with a collection of young boys. Women gossiped by the food table as the men examined the targets for a turkey shoot.

Travis pressed his hand into the small of Meredith's back as he guided her into the crowd. She hesitated when she saw the hand-painted banner tacked up between two trees that read, "Welcome, Doctor."

Travis trailed her gaze. "I didn't realize the new doctor was coming so soon."

She shrugged a delicate shoulder. "There didn't seem much point."

"When did the town council expect you out of your house?" He felt his own anger rising.

"Month's end."

"This month? That's less than two weeks." He couldn't believe they were forcing her out of her home. "Where were you going to go?"

"Likely to the Harpers'. They'd offered me a room."

She deserved better than a rented room.

Meredith fiddled with the buttons at her neckline as she drank in the lively fiddle music. "I've never seen such a turnout."

He wasn't fooled by her light tone. Meredith's life had changed and she was afraid. "The new doctor can't be as good as you."

She shrugged, but he saw stiffness in her shoulders. "He's likely got a lot of good education that I never had. And the town does need a real doctor."

He squeezed her hand. "But you care like no one else I've ever met."

She did care. And the fact reinforced what he'd come to believe—she never would have knowingly hurt the men in Libby. It wasn't in her makeup. Whatever she'd done those years ago had not been intentional.

An elderly woman approached Meredith. Her body was withered, her shoulders hunched, but her eyes were bright.

"Meredith Carter! I want to speak to you."

Meredith's smile was warm. "Mrs. Tupper. Good to see you up and about. You're looking spry."

She waved away Meredith's words. "Edith Harper says you got married to some Yank. I say she's crazy."

"I did get married."

Mrs. Tupper was not the least intimidated by Travis, though he outweighed her by a hundred pounds and stood over a foot taller. "I heard about you. Edith says you saved Meredith."

Travis shifted his shoulders under his jacket. News in this town spread like wildfire. "She saved me, too."

"Heard about that, too." She waggled a bony finger at Travis. "You mind yourself, boy. Be good to Meredith or I'll put a hex on you."

Travis nodded gravely. "I'll do right by her."

"See that you do."

A tall man with a lean, muscular build cut through the crowd with quiet but determined purpose. He wore blue pants and a white shirt cuffed at his wrists. He looked as staid and stiff as any shopkeeper. They'd not been formally introduced, but Travis knew who he was. George Walker.

"Meredith," Walker said, taking her hand.

She squeezed his hand affectionately. "George."

"I hear congratulations are in order." If Walker was angry or disappointed, he didn't show it. "You really got married?"

"Yes." She hesitated, as if the words caught in her throat. "Meet my husband, Captain Travis Rafferty."

Walker held out his hand and Travis accepted it. The shopkeeper's handshake was stronger than he expected and his gaze piercingly direct. "You're a lucky man, Rafferty."

"I know."

"Take care of her."

How many people were going to issue the same warning? "I will."

George studied him a moment longer then cleared his throat. "Mind if I dance with your bride, Rafferty? I promise to bring her back."

He'd just as soon have told the man to get lost. "Sure."

Meredith accepted George's hand. They moved toward the stand where the men played their fiddles, and joined the other couples already dancing. Walker said something to Meredith and she laughed.

Travis ground his teeth.

He tried not to glare at Meredith and the shopkeeper. Instead, he moved to the refreshment table and let a woman put a cup of punch in his hand.

The chatter of people buzzed around his head. The women stared at him, but none had the nerve to strike up a conversation and he made no effort to talk to them. He didn't have a taste for punch or this crowd.

His temper warmed from a simmer to a boil when a rancher approached the dancing couple and tapped George on the shoulder. The storekeeper didn't look happy, but he stepped back and allowed the other man to take Meredith in his arms and dance.

Travis stood by the large campfire, where a pig roasted, and he watched as another three men cut in and danced with Meredith.

His wife was full of life, loved by all and he could hardly believe she was his now.

His future.

He reached inside his coat pocket and pulled out the small journal he'd kept infrequently over the years. From the middle page he pulled out the list he'd carefully made during the weeks after his escape.

He studied the list of the dead men. There was a lingering sadness, which likely would never go away, but for the first time the rage had abated. Meredith had been right. His men had been like

James. Young, good men who'd been cheated out of a full life.

The time had come to let them go and release the guilt he'd harbored for years.

He tossed the list into the fire and watched the flames lap around the edges then burn through the yellowing paper. In seconds, the list vanished into the cinders.

Travis tucked his journal back into his pocket and searched the dance area for Meredith. It was time to claim his wife.

He strode past the couples toward Meredith. He tapped her unsuspecting partner on the shoulder. The man whipped his head around as if he'd argue, took one long look at Travis and stepped back.

Travis didn't speak as he swept Meredith into his arms and started to move in time with the music. She felt so damn good, fit against him as if they were made for each other.

She looked up at him, amusement twinkling in her eyes. "You weren't very nice to Lannie."

His temper was cooling. Life shifted back into place with her in his arms. "Who?"

"My dance partner."

"I didn't like what he was thinking when he was looking at you."

Her eyes sparkled with interest. "How do you know what he was thinking?"

"I'm a man. We all think alike when it comes to a beautiful woman like you."

She laughed. "Lannie is just a friend. He'd never think of me that way."

He spun her around. "He'd have to be dead not to."

They moved in time with the music and he held her close. He noted the ring of men on the dance floor staring at him as if he were a poacher. "So who else was in the running?"

"For what?" She relaxed into him.

She smelled good. "You."

"You make it sound like I'm the prize in a race."

"You are a prize."

She studied his face. "We did make the right decision, didn't we?"

"Yes." He squeezed her arms tighter.

When the music stopped, he didn't let her go. For the first time in years, the unanswered questions didn't nag him as they once had. The mystery regarding the failed escape likely would never be solved. And he was willing to accept that.

The moment of peace left as quickly as it had come.

Horse hooves pounded the dirt, echoing across the rolling grasslands to the east. Everyone turned to face the sound, smiles on their faces as they expected to see the stage that carried the new doctor. Instead, ten horsemen, dressed in Union uniforms, thundered into town.

The soldiers looked travel weary, as if they'd been on the trail for days. The one exception was the young officer who led the pack. He sat tall and straight in his saddle and wore his uniform as if it had been tailor-made. The sun glistened on his black boots and his blond hair graced the top of his starched collar.

Travis couldn't believe it.

Captain Ward dismounted. He tugged his coat in place and adjusted his hat as he scanned the crowd. Almost immediately, his gaze cut Travis and Meredith from the crowd.

Chapter Fifteen

Meredith could hardly believe the tall, slim soldier was Michael Ward, the man she'd treated in Libby Prison. Then he'd been wallowing in filth with barely enough strength to lift his head. His skin had been sallow and his eyes distant and cloudy. He'd been dying.

Now he was the picture of health. He walked with ease and grace and wore his neatly pressed uniform like a true war hero.

Meredith noticed that several of the young girls blushed as he passed and whispered excitedly to each other.

To her surprise, Travis didn't greet Ward. His stance was rigid and his fists clenched at his side.

If Ward noted Travis's tension, he gave no hint of it. He grinned broadly, revealing even, white teeth as he tugged off his glove and extended his hand to Travis. "Captain Rafferty! You're a hard man to find."

Travis accepted Ward's hand, but his stance remained rigid, suspicious. "Ward. I'm surprised to see you."

Instead of responding to Travis, Captain Ward swung his gaze to Meredith. "Is this Meredith Carter?"

"Yes," Travis growled.

He took her hand. His grip was light and his palm smooth. "I was a bit indisposed when we first met."

Something in the smooth, cultured voice put her senses on alert. She edged closer to Travis. "You were quite ill."

"Yes, I was." He held up his hand and flexed his fingers. His thumb, index finger and middle fingers moved, but his ring finger and pinky were as rigid as wood. "Sadly, I never regained full range of motion in my fingers. And my arm still pains me when it rains, but I am grateful. Many a man in my position could have lost the arm or died."

"I'm glad I could help."

Ward's deep blue gaze studied her face. "That night you were little more than a blur to me, but

I had no idea how lovely you are. I see why the men called you an angel.''

The fiddle music and dancing had stopped. The crowd, now quiet, had gathered around, silent and watching.

''Ward, what are you doing here?''

''I came to help you,'' Ward said, after tearing his gaze from Meredith.

Travis's shoulders straightened another fraction. ''I didn't ask for help.''

Ward flashed his white teeth. ''I thought you'd need help finding Mrs. Carter.''

''As you can see, I found her.''

''So I see. Excellent work.''

Fear slithered down Meredith's spine. ''None of this makes sense.''

Ward tugged his left glove back over his partially paralyzed hand. ''You've become quite a celebrity back East. The newspapers have picked up your story.''

''How'd they find out?'' Travis demanded.

''Can't say. There's always someone willing to talk to see their name in print.'' He let his words settle before he added, ''That's why the men and I will escort you back to Washington. Between the Indians and the Reb renegades, it's a dangerous trip home.''

Her fingernails dug into her palm. Something about the way Ward spoke set her nerves on edge.

Travis must have sensed it, too. "I don't need your help. Meredith is my responsibility."

Ward's eyes remained friendly. "Not anymore."

Sheriff Harper pushed through the crowd. "Now what is going on?"

"And you are…?" Ward seemed accustomed to smoothing feathers.

"Sheriff Fox Harper."

Ward nodded. "Sheriff Harper, excellent you should be in on this conversation. I like to keep local law enforcement informed."

Ward removed a neat, crisply folded piece of paper from his breast pocket. "Before Captain Rafferty left Washington, he came to me regarding an incident that happened during the war. Are you familiar with what I'm talking about?"

"Captain Rafferty explained it all," the sheriff said.

"Excellent. So you must realize, as a man sworn to uphold the law, that this kind of complaint cannot go ignored. Men died during that escape attempt."

Meredith wavered between fear and anger. "I had nothing to do with it."

A humorless smile tugged the hard edges of Ward's mouth. "Mrs. Carter, I conducted my own investigation into the matter after Captain Rafferty came to me."

Travis stiffened. "I think the guard lied, Ward."

Ward tugged the edge of his glove over his cuff. "There's more evidence, Rafferty."

Meredith felt as if she were drowning in mud. "You couldn't have. I didn't do anything wrong!"

Travis's eyes flashed with challenge and worry. "It must be substantial to bring you out here."

Ward shook his head. "Your investigation opened a hornet's nest. Families, some very prominent, of the men who died in the prison escape heard of your quest for justice. They are putting a lot of pressure on Washington to see that the traitor—namely Mrs. Meredith Carter—is brought to justice."

Sheriff Harper spit on the ground. "This ain't got nothing to do with justice."

Travis held up his hand to silence the old man. "Say what you have to say, Ward."

The younger man shrugged and shifted his gaze to Meredith. "Mrs. Carter—you are under arrest."

* * *

Meredith swallowed her terror as she stared at the ring of mounted soldiers. There were at least a dozen, and all were heavily armed and glaring at her as if she'd already been tried and convicted.

Travis's expression was inscrutable. "Meredith has already agreed to return under my escort."

Ward fanned his hand toward the soldiers. "Excellent. Then there'll be no trouble, because we all want the same thing."

Travis didn't speak.

Ward fingered the brass button on his cuff. "I am only here to make your journey easier. We will all take Mrs. Carter to Washington together."

Travis's face was hard, unyielding. She had the image of the battlefield soldier, mounted, facing the enemy and ready to engage.

"When do you want to leave, Captain Ward?" her new husband asked.

Meredith's heart hammered in her chest. What was he saying? She trusted Travis, not Ward, to bring her back East.

Ward relaxed, a man in control. "Now suits."

Mrs. Harper objected. "You can't take her today. We're welcoming the new doctor."

"That hardly concerns me," Ward said.

"Mrs. Carter is a respected member of the

community," Travis said coolly. "The folks here want Mrs. Carter and the doctor to meet."

Ward lifted an eyebrow. "So where is this new doctor?"

"He hasn't arrived," Mrs. Harper said.

Ward's lips flattened with impatience. "When will he be here?"

"Can't say. An hour, maybe more." Mrs. Harper shrugged.

"A few more hours won't make a difference," Travis said.

Ward stared at the solemn, angry faces of the townsfolk for the first time. His smile wavered.

Meredith guessed he wasn't the kind of man who made enemies unless he had to. He'd bide his time for now, but they'd be on their way before daybreak.

"Fine," Ward said. "My men have ridden hard and they could use a break."

"Of course," Travis said. "There's a livery at the other end of town if you need to water your horses."

"Thank you."

Travis managed a smile that didn't reach his eyes. "Sheriff, why don't you tell those fiddlers to start playing again?"

"Fine," the old man grumbled. "Though no one is gonna feel much like dancing anymore."

Once Ward and his men started for the livery, the fiddle music started up. Folks, stunned by the soldiers' arrival, broke into small groups and started talking among themselves. No one danced.

Meredith opened her mouth to speak to Travis, but he took her by the arm, silencing her. He marched her back to the boardwalk. The Harpers stayed on their trail.

Her nerves tightened another notch. "Travis, what is going on? Why would Ward ride all the way to Texas to find me? It doesn't make sense."

Travis rubbed the back of his neck as he watched the soldiers disappear around the corner. "I don't know and I don't like it."

She watched the muscle work in his jaw. "Why didn't you tell them we were married?"

He laid his hands on her shoulders. "Because I wanted to keep our options open."

"What options?" Mrs. Harper said.

"Escape." Both Travis and Sheriff Harper spoke in unison.

Meredith shook her head. "I'm not afraid to go back, Travis, as long as you're with me."

Travis swallowed. "Ward's arrival changes everything. I don't know what kind of evidence he has against you, but it could be substantial.''

Unease flickered through her limbs. She sensed Travis's worry. "Surely it won't stand up.''

"It could be very damning, Meredith. More dangerous than we realize.''

Something cold tightened her insides. "We'll face it together.''

He brushed a lock of hair from her forehead. "It's better if we get on our horses and ride out of town.''

"What about your career in the military?''

"There are other jobs. It's more important that you're safe. We can disappear. Colorado Territory maybe.''

Mentally she dug in her heels. "I don't want to run from this.''

"You don't have a choice.'' He looked weary. Something about the tone of his voice struck her. A chill rushed through her veins.

"But I am innocent. You believe that, don't you? You said before we married that you trusted me.''

"I do. I trust you to be there for me. I trust you to care for our children. I trust we can build a life together.''

"But do you trust that I kept your secret?''

Travis's face was a mixture of pain and longing. "You're a good woman, Meredith. I don't want anything to happen to you."

"You didn't answer my question." She pulled away from him. Her heart clenched.

He flexed his fingers as if finding the right words were a struggle. "The war was a hard time for us all."

She edged back. "But you believe I betrayed you."

"It's not as simple as that."

"Yes, it is. You either believe in my innocence or you do not."

He took her hands in his. "I believe, whatever you did, you didn't intentionally mean to hurt anyone."

She jerked her hands free. Her head started to spin. Whatever fragile hopes she harbored for the future shattered in an instant. "You think I told someone about the prison escape."

"Meredith—" he pleaded.

The look on his face was too much to bear. "Yes or no!" she shouted.

He reached out to her. "Meredith, we need to talk."

"I was such a fool," she whispered. "Such a fool."

If she looked at his face another moment, she feared she'd break into a thousand pieces. In a panic, she fled, away from the party down the Main Street without a care as to where she was going. She only knew she wanted to get away from Travis.

Travis nearly crumpled when he saw Meredith's face. In that moment, he *knew* that he'd been wrong about her.

She *had* been innocent.

He'd been such a blind fool, willing to forgive her for something she'd never done. He'd have laughed at the irony if the situation wasn't so dire.

"Meredith!" He started after her. If the soldiers saw her running, they'd assume she was trying to escape.

Before he could catch her, she ran headlong into a Union soldier that Ward must have left posted near the party. For an instant, she stared up at the guard, as if her mind didn't process the fact that she'd run into the soldier.

"You can't leave town, miss." The soldier's gravelly voice held no malice.

"I have to get away," she said. Her voice sounded weak, broken.

The soldier's face hardened. "You've got to

stay in view of the soldiers, miss. Captain Ward wants you back in Washington, no matter what.''

Travis reached for Meredith and took her by the arm. She tried to free herself but he wouldn't release her. "I'll take it from here, Sergeant."

"Let go of me," she shouted. "I never want to see you again."

"Meredith," Travis said tersely. "Be quiet. We need to talk."

She tried to twist her arm free. "Let me go!"

"Ma'am, you can't leave," the soldier said.

The commotion caught Ward's attention. He stopped midstride on his way to the livery, turned and looked at Meredith. His eyes narrowed.

The hair on the back of Travis's neck rose as it always did before an ambush.

Ward cut away from his men and started back toward them. "What little drama is this?"

Travis stiffened. "Nothing. Mrs. Carter and I simply need to talk."

She brushed the tears from her face and raised her chin. "We're finished talking, Captain Rafferty."

Ward eyes narrowed. "Was she trying to leave town, Sergeant?"

The soldier shifted as if uncomfortable. "I don't believe so, sir. She looked upset."

Ward's blue eyes hardened. He possessed a cunning edge that belied his youthful features. "She certainly has reason enough to run."

Sheriff Harper strode forward. His face was grim, his hand resting on his gun. "Mrs. Carter wasn't going anywhere."

Ward shook his head. "I disagree."

Travis swallowed a growl. Why did Ward care so damn much, when two months ago he didn't want to be bothered with "ancient history"?

Sheriff Harper rested his hand on his gun. "She's just upset."

Meredith lifted her chin. "I am not upset. In fact, I am thinking clearer than I have in weeks." She swung her gaze on Ward. "I want to prove to everyone that I am innocent."

Travis's gut tightened as if he'd been punched. She sounded so proud, and so defeated.

Sheriff Harper leveled his gaze on Travis. "Meredith, we've been all through this."

Meredith shook her head. "It's time to put this to an end once and for all."

It was as if she'd lost—no, he'd stolen—her will to fight. Travis knew she'd given up, but he had not. He vowed to protect her until they got this mess sorted out.

Several people in the crowd voiced their displeasure. Others started to move closer, as if to say Meredith wasn't going anywhere.

Travis studied the crowd. They were the leverage he needed right now. "Ward, better to wait until morning, when you haven't got an audience."

Ward quickly assessed. "All right. We leave in the morning. But she spends the night in jail."

Sheriff Harper, visibly relieved, took Meredith's arm. "I'll keep a close eye on her."

Ward nodded. "I'll also have one of my men posted outside the prison."

Silently Travis followed Meredith and the stone-faced sheriff to jail. It nearly broke his heart to see her step into the cell and move to the cot. When the cell door clanged shut, she flinched.

His mind raced through facts surrounding the escape. Something wasn't adding up.

I'll get you out.

We'll work this out.

"Travis," she said softly.

It took everything in him to keep the emotion from his voice. "Yes?"

"When this is over, I never want to see you again."

Chapter Sixteen

Hours after sunset, Meredith sat on the edge of her cot, her back to the wall and her feet tucked under her skirt. The air in the cell had cooled.

She felt numb, as if her body wasn't quite her own. She pressed her head against her knees

There'd been no sight of Travis for over six hours. Her mind was relieved she didn't have to face him, but her heart ached.

He didn't believe in her.

The words played over and over in her head, crushing her heart and sapping her will to fight. She didn't care what happened to her now.

Sheriff Harper sat at his desk polishing his gun. He kept trying to strike up conversations with her, but she'd not had the energy to speak. She'd simply wanted to be alone, to curl up in a ball and forget about the world.

Meredith had never felt so alone. So tired.

"Meredith," the sheriff said. "Can I get you an extra blanket?"

She shook her head. "No, thanks."

"How about something to eat? I don't think you've eaten since this morning."

The dear man was trying and for that she'd always be grateful. "I'm not very hungry."

Suddenly the door to the jailhouse opened. Her head jerked up.

Travis stood in the doorway. He was dressed to ride. He wore his range coat, leather gloves, guns and hat low on his head.

Despite the hurt and anger, her heart leapt. Lord, but she loved the man. And she'd have traded just about anything to have him believe in her.

Meredith rose from the cot and moved to the barred door. "I don't want to see you."

Travis didn't look at Meredith. Instead his gaze was focused on the sheriff. "Harper, can you give me some time alone with Meredith?"

She gripped the bars until her knuckles whitened. "Fox Harper, don't leave me alone with him."

The sheriff stood, rubbing his hands on the stiff muscles of his thigh. He glanced at Meredith then turned back to Travis. "I ain't never seen her this upset before."

"I'll set things right."

"See that you do."

He reached for his hat. "I'm surprised the guard outside let you in."

"He's napping."

The sheriff chuckled. "He just came on duty. He shouldn't be tired."

Travis shrugged. "Your wife was kind enough to give him coffee—with a little of that tooth medicine mixed in it."

A sly grin slid over the old man's face. "And they call me Fox. He'll be out for hours."

"Sheriff, don't you dare leave," Meredith shouted.

The sheriff stretched. "I need a break, Meredith. Need to move my legs." He looked at Travis, his eyes full of meaning. "Take care of her."

"I will."

Meredith smacked the iron bars. "Fox Harper, don't do this to me."

He tipped his hat to her. "Reckon, it's the best thing I could do for you. You two got some talking to do."

Panic exploded inside her. She loved Travis

with her whole heart and feared she'd not have the resolve to resist him. "I have nothing to say to him."

The sheriff opened the door. "You'll think of something."

As the door slammed shut, she backed away from the bars. "You, stay away from me!"

Travis scooped the iron ring of keys off the desk. His face was tight, determined. "I heard the guards talking. They are coming for you an hour after sunup. They're taking you back. But I'm not going to let that happen."

"I told you I wouldn't run from this."

He strode across the room. "We can ride west. There are places we can hide."

If his words were meant to comfort her, they didn't. In fact it made her feel worse. Hadn't he said that the guilty run? "I'm not running!"

He shoved the key in the lock and pinned her with his gaze. "I know when a battle can be won, and when it can't. This battle of yours in Washington can't be won."

She curled her fingers into fists. "But I am innocent."

He turned the key until the lock clicked. "I know that."

His casually spoken words were sweeter than

any she'd ever heard. She felt her defenses drop for an instant. ''No, you don't!''

Sadness and regret filled his eyes. ''I made a mistake, Meredith, when I didn't trust you.''

Oh, how she wanted to believe that. But trust didn't come easily. ''What changed your mind about me?'' she said, bitterness dripping from her words. ''Find the evidence you needed?''

He pushed open the door but didn't approach, as if she were a skittish colt that would bolt if he tried to touch her. ''I've been a fool, Meredith. I know now that you are a woman of your word. I've seen it over and over again, but was too blind to accept it.''

She wavered and had to steel herself against the tide of happiness that threatened to wash away reason. ''I don't believe you.''

He didn't enter the cell. ''The night you saved my life, I knew, deep down, you were innocent. It just took my pride time to catch up with my brain.''

Despite her best efforts, the cold feeling around her heart started to lift. ''How will I ever know you truly believe in me?''

''Faith,'' he said simply.

Her throat tightened.

"We've got to learn to trust each other, Meredith."

"I want to believe you."

"It's all about trust." He held out his hand. "I trust you. Do you trust me?"

He was asking her to believe in him when there was no proof, just as she'd been asking him to believe in her. In some strange, unexplainable way, she did believe him. All the barriers crumbled and she rushed into his arms. She closed the distance between them and took his hand.

He wrapped his strong arms around her shoulders, then pulled her against his chest.

"I can face anything now," she whispered.

He pulled back so that he could see her face. "You're not facing anything. We're still leaving tonight."

She gripped his arms. "We can prove my innocence together."

"Like I said—we have to fall back."

"You'd be giving up everything if we run."

He smoothed the hair from her eyes. "No, I'd be gaining everything. You're all I've got in the world, Meredith, and I don't want to lose you."

Sadness drained her short-lived joy. "If you run, your career—your future—will be ruined."

"It won't mean anything if you're rotting in a Federal prison."

Her heart pumped with fear and excitement. The idea of starting a new life with Travis was tempting. Together they could build a fine life together out West, where it was easy to get lost in the prairies and mountains.

It was a beautiful dream.

But it was wrong.

"I'm not going with you," she whispered.

He looked at her as if she'd gone mad. "What?"

A calm had washed over her. "I'm not running from this, Travis. You and I both know that it would haunt us for the rest of our lives."

Frustrated, he glared at her. "It's something we can live with."

"Is it? Honor is the center of your life."

He gripped her shoulders. "*You* are the center of my life."

"We have to settle this once and for all. Surely, there has to be a way we can find out what Ward is about."

Travis tightened his grip. "Believe me, I've thought it all through. I spoke to the telegraph officer about the message the gunman received."

"Mr. Dickenson?"

"Yes. He said the message was sent from St. Louis. It's a dead end."

Her heart sank, but she refused to show her disappointment. "There must be something else we can do."

"There's nothing." His sharp gaze held hers and then he crushed her against him as if he were afraid she'd vanish.

"We must have faith it will work out."

He stared down at her. His honor and desires warred inside him. He pulled away from her and stared out the window. Thousands of stars flickered in the black sky. He didn't speak for a long moment. "They're coming for you just after sunup."

She came up behind him and wrapped her arms around his waist. She pressed her cheek against his back. "I'm not afraid as long as I have you."

He turned and cupped her face in his hands. "I don't want to lose you. I've spent a lifetime alone." He hesitated. "I couldn't go back to that kind of isolation."

"You're not." She stood on tiptoe and kissed his forehead.

"I'll be with you every step of the way."

"I know."

Meredith stared into his blue eyes, the color of cut sapphires. Lord, but she loved him.

She touched his strong chin. The thick stubble teased her fingers and sent a shiver dancing down her spine. Touching him made her feel alive.

She stared at his full lips, suddenly wanting him to kiss her. Not because she was afraid, but because she yearned to again taste the dark, sensual emotions he'd introduced her to. She had never wanted a man so much, not like this, not so completely.

"Make love to me," she whispered.

A grin tugged the corner of his mouth. "We've a division of soldiers out there."

She pulled his hat off and tossed it on the floor. "And we're in here all alone."

He shrugged off his coat and then pulled her roughly against him. His lips, hot and hungry, covered her mouth as he crushed her against his chest. The whirl of sensations overpowered her and for an instant she couldn't summon a single thought.

She released all her fears, all her worries and surrendered herself to the sensation.

She felt so alive. So alive.

He lowered her to the cot, his warrior's hands moving over her body, plundering her senses.

Low, throaty whispers escaped her throat. She arched against him.

Travis unfastened the buttons that trailed between her breasts and pushed the calico fabric aside. Her white, creamy breasts, barely veiled by the thin cotton chemise, glistened in the moonlight.

She moved her hands from her breasts, inviting him. He didn't hesitate.

Knowing this could be the last time they made love for a very long time heightened the sensations. The pleasure was both bitter and sweet.

He suckled her through the fabric. Growing more impatient for the feel of her skin, he pushed her bodice open and kissed her naked breasts. He trailed kisses down her flat stomach, and then licked the smooth skin of her belly.

Hungry for more, he started to move lower. An unsteady laugh tumbled out of her. She was torn between pure delight and shame as she dug her fingers into his hair and arched her back. "What are you doing?"

"You'll see," he said, his voice rough and ripe with passion. He pushed her skirts up, bunching them at her hips then tugged her pantaloons down.

What he did next shocked, stunned and utterly

delighted her. She opened her legs for him, as she gripped the cot's rough blanket in her hands.

She'd never imagined it would be like this. It had been wondrous before when they'd made love, but now it was so overpowering. There wasn't the uncertainty of the first time, only a throbbing desire.

Several times he brought her close to the edge, but each time he skillfully changed tactics so that he had her whimpering from the exquisite torture.

Travis rose, unfastened his pants and quickly pushed them down. She moistened her lips as she stared at his erection.

Before the fires inside her could cool even a degree, he was on top of her again, kissing, stealing her control, driving her half-mad with wanting.

Her insides were on fire, her body moist with wanting. "Travis, don't make me wait any longer."

He did not delay this time. His own control strained to the breaking point. He drove inside her.

Meredith wrapped her legs around him, taking in all of him. Her fingers trembled as she cupped his buttocks and stroked the taut muscles of his back.

He started to move inside her, his thrusts urgent. She strained to meet him, savoring the timeless dance of lovers.

And then, without warning, the fire inside of them exploded. It radiated through every fiber of their bodies and utterly consumed them.

Later, she woke to darkness. She didn't know what time it was, but shadows still cut across the walls and the moon remained high in the sky. She was aware that Travis was beside her. Their bodies were spooned together on the narrow cot.

His breathing was deep, even and gave her comfort.

They'd crossed a threshold tonight. He'd not spoken of love, but there was trust. They would build on that, and if he never grew to love her, she had enough for both of them.

Ward couldn't sleep with so much at stake. Wearing only his undershirt, pants and suspenders, he crossed his tent and dug the soft, clean muslin rag from his saddlebag. He sat down on his cot and started to polish the already glistening belt buckle.

Appearances were so important. Hadn't his Roberta—his dear Robbie—said so over and over?

Many of the men in the field had forgotten that. They let the dust cake on their boots, allowed their uniforms to become sweat stained and filthy. Not him. His father had raised him to be the perfect soldier and he had vowed long ago never to disappoint.

Ward paused for a moment and closed his eyes. His career, his life, all teetered on the edge of destruction because of one mistake. He hadn't wanted to tell the guards about the prison escape. But he'd had no choice. He had been in so much pain and he knew if he'd stayed in that hellhole another week, he'd have died.

Rafferty had given him hope during the hours after he'd been shot. He'd gotten the doctor to dig the bullet out and arranged for the medicine that had melted the fire in his blood.

But in the end, Rafferty had left him. Left him to die and fend for himself.

Ward rubbed the buckle's brass until a blister formed on his thumb. "It wasn't my fault. Rafferty gave me no choice."

He remembered how the men had trailed out through the tunnel. How their lantern light had grown dimmer and dimmer and how the panic had tightened around his heart until he thought it would burst.

He'd summoned the guard—and traded information for freedom.

He squeezed his eyes shut. He'd never intended things to go so sour. He'd never meant for all those men to die.

For a moment, the present faded and the past whirled around him. All he could hear were the gunshots, the screams and the growling dogs.

His hands started to tremble and his body sweated. He pressed the buckle to his forehead and leaned forward, rocking gently back and forth.

When he'd returned to Washington after his imprisonment, he'd blamed Meredith for the failed escape. The wife of a rebel, everyone was eager to believe she'd sold the men out.

He'd been called a hero for surviving Libby and the gunshot. For the first time in his career, his father had pronounced him worthy of the uniform.

For a time, everything had been perfect.

Then Rafferty had stirred the hornet's nest with his questions and his foolish sense of honor. He'd been bound and determined to bring Mrs. Carter back, to have her testify for all.

Ward stretched his stiff shoulder and flexed the fingers of his right hand. The fingertips were numb and the soreness in the muscles seemed worse than normal.

The discomfort and inconvenience of the old wound were reminders of the war—ones that he could live with.

Meredith Carter was a reminder he couldn't live with.

Her very existence threatened his and his wife's position in Washington, his very future.

The sooner Meredith Carter died, the better.

There was a knock at the tent's entrance.

Ward's head snapped up. "I said I didn't want to be disturbed."

Rafferty pushed open the tent flap and stepped into the tent. "I want to make a deal."

Hours later, Meredith awoke again. This time the dewy haze of lovemaking had passed and the first rays of morning light trickled into the cell, casting an eerie glow onto her rumpled skirts.

She stretched, more content than she'd ever been. Swinging her legs over the side of the cot, she looked around the cell and jailhouse for Travis.

His scent still clung to her, but her body had grown cold. She wanted to see him, touch him, feel his heartbeat next to her skin.

Standing, she moved to the cell bars. The door was locked.

There was the subtle shift of movement in the corner near the desk. Fear prickled down her spine. "Sheriff Harper?"

From the shadows stepped the long, lean frame of Captain Ward. "Good morning, angel."

Chapter Seventeen

Meredith choked down the terror rising in her throat. "What are you doing here?"

Ward's smile was cool, controlled. "It's time to go."

"Now? So early?" Her gaze skittered over the jailhouse. They were alone. "Where is the sheriff and Captain Rafferty?"

"The sheriff and the guard I posted are on break. I told them both to get something to eat, that I would look after you."

Her mind raced. "Where is Captain Rafferty?"

"Captain Rafferty won't be back for a good hour. I sent him on an errand."

Panic clogged her throat. "What kind of errand?"

"Back to your homestead. I ordered him to take a few men and burn it to the ground."

She fisted her fingers. "He wouldn't do that!"

"He would. He's the kind of man who knows where his loyalties lie."

Her head spun. "They're not with you."

He turned the key and the lock clicked open. "I thought you might like to go for a walk before we rode out."

She moved to the far corner of the cell and pressed her back against the wall. "I want to wait for the sheriff and Captain Rafferty."

Confidently, he stepped into the cell. "You're going for a walk."

"Captain Rafferty wouldn't leave me alone like this."

"Of course he would. He's a man who knows his priorities."

"What are you talking about?"

He jangled the keys in his hand. "He came to me last night. Told me everything. He told me about the men who'd come to your ranch and shot him. How you saved his life." His eyes narrowed. "How he had you last night."

Suddenly she felt sick and dizzy. "No."

His sharp blue gaze bored into her. "We had

quite a laugh over that—how you gave yourself to him.''

Tears brimmed in her eyes. Travis never would have spoken to Ward about something that had been so private. ''I don't believe you.''

He leaned a fraction closer. ''Tell me, Meredith. Did he make you scream out his name?''

She shrank back. ''You are disgusting.''

He took a step closer to her. ''No, just a man, who, like every other man in Libby Prison, dreamed about you every night for months and months after your visit. You are a beauty. And all this is such a waste.''

A cold chill snaked down her spine. ''What are you talking about?''

He reached for his gloves and, with deliberate slowness, put them on. ''Don't make this hard. If you cooperate, I promise to make it quick.''

She searched frantically around the cell for any way out. Nothing. Where was Travis? ''Make what quick?''

''Your death.''

The pieces tumbled into place. Ward had betrayed his own men. He reached out and snagged her wrist. His grip was surprisingly strong. He yanked her out of the cell so hard she tripped and fell to her knees. "Why? I saved your life."

He lifted her to her feet. "And for that I will always be grateful." He sucked in a breath. "Meredith, I don't like this any better than you do, but I simply can't risk you going back to Washington and telling your story. Those doe eyes of yours could easily sway a jury."

"I won't tell anyone anything if you let me go."

He pushed her toward the door. "You're going to do what you do best. You're going to tell them the truth. You see, I know you didn't betray those prisoners. But it's important to me that others keep believing you did."

She whirled around and plastered her back to the door. Travis!

"Why did you do it?" she whispered.

He shoved a shaky hand through his hair. "My father and grandfather have a long history in the army. They're heroes and they pumped me full of honor and glory. But I never expected to be in that damn prison camp for so long. I never expected to be so cold or so hungry. It's easy to talk about glory when you're warm and your belly is full. And then I got shot. The pain was unbearable. And I didn't care about honor anymore, I just wanted out.''

"That's why you weren't there the next day when I came back. They'd released you in exchange for information.''

He shook his head. "It was meant to be a simple transaction. No one was supposed to die.''

"Seventeen men died that night. You killed your own men.''

Anger flashed in his eyes. "No, I did not! The Rebs killed those men. They weren't supposed to shoot. They were just supposed to round them up, bring them back. No one was supposed to die.''

"You blamed me.''

"It was the perfect solution. No one cared about you. And I honestly thought it would end with that one white lie. And it would have if not for Rafferty. He had to know what happened.''

"What about the guard in Richmond?''

"I paid him. He'd have blamed it on his mother for the right amount of money.''

The room started to swim. "What are you going to do with me now?''

"Like I said, we are going for a little walk. You are going to run, try to escape. And I will be forced to shoot you.''

"I won't do it."

"Yes, you will."

"No! I won't. I won't run."

He looked almost bored. "The Harpers are nice people. I'd hate to see a terrible accident befall them."

"No!" Tears spilled down her face. "Please don't hurt them. You don't have to do any of this. I won't speak of the war ever again."

"I can't take that risk." He tapped his foot. "You know this is Rafferty's fault. If he'd just left well enough alone. But he didn't. Had to be the hero, had to right a wrong that, in the big scheme of things, meant nothing to anyone of importance."

"He wanted justice for his men."

"What about me? If it got out what I'd done, I'd be ruined. Father would be so angry. And my wife Roberta had great plans for me."

The unexpected gunmen, her ruined house—it all made sense. "You sent those killers. You ransacked my house."

"When my little friends didn't report back, I realized they'd botched the job. I went to your cabin, ready to kill you myself. I did become a little angry when I discovered you weren't there. This has all been such a frustrating mess. Father has plans for me to be a general, you know.''

"Captain, please."

Ward drew his gun and motioned her forward. "It's still early and if we hurry we can take care of business before anyone's the wiser. No one gets hurt. Except you, of course."

Meredith glanced around. "Captain, you don't have to do this."

He raised his gun. "Don't make this difficult. I've enough bad memories to last a lifetime. Now open the door."

Seeing no choice, Meredith turned slowly and lifted the latch. With leaden feet, she walked around to the back of the jailhouse as Ward indicated. There, she saw the guard and Sheriff Harper. They were knocked out cold.

Meredith's stomach lurched when she saw the trail of blood oozing down the sheriff's face. "I need to help him."

Ward hurried her past him. "He'll be fine. Just a bump on the head. I made sure to get them both from behind, so they didn't know who hit them. Later, that'll also be blamed on you."

She stumbled, tripped and fell into the dirt.

"Get up," he snapped.

"No! You'll have to kill me here before I run."

He leaned over her. "How about if I just shoot your arm, maybe an elbow. That might motivate you a little."

She scooped up handfuls of dirt. "I won't run again!"

A shot rang out, catching Ward in his hand. He yelped and dropped his gun. Rafferty and two other Union officers stepped out of the shadows. "Move away from her, Ward."

Ward's gaze turned feral. "How dare you!" He looked to the other soldiers. "He shot me. Did you men see that? He shot me. Do something."

The soldiers didn't move, their faces hard masks.

As quick as a mountain lion, Ward jerked Meredith off the ground and, from his gun belt, removed a small derringer. "I ordered you to go to the cabin and burn it."

Travis kept his voice even, void of emotion. "I know where my loyalties lie."

Ward pulled Meredith closer to him. "With her? She's nothing but a dirty spy. She sent your men to their deaths."

Travis shook his head. "No, Ward, she did not. You did."

"Liar!" Ward shouted.

His gaze was trained on Ward, not her. "The men and I heard it all. There's no need for any more lying."

Ward's body went rigid. "I should have had her killed years ago. But she left for Texas. I didn't want any more bloodshed and I wanted to be fair."

Travis's face paled. "Let her go."

Ward poked the gun harder against her skin, making her wince. "No. She's coming with me. Now, drop your guns. This little gun of mine doesn't make a big hole, but I'll wager it does a fair amount of damage to her skull."

Travis and the soldiers hesitated.

Meredith tried to move her head away from the tip of the barrel, but Ward savagely drove it deeper into her skin.

"Do it!" Ward screeched.

Travis held up his palm and gun in surrender. Slowly he and the other men squatted and laid their weapons down. "Calm down, Ward."

"Calm down?" Ward wailed. "How am I supposed to calm down? Thanks to you, I've not only got to kill her but you and two Union officers. This is turning into one mess.''

"It doesn't have to be this way.'' The lines around Travis's face and eyes deepened.

"And how would you suggest it end, Captain? I can't go back to Washington with this kind of incident on my record. It has to be cleaned up.'' He forced himself to think. "Captain, kick the gun over here.''

Travis's jaw tightened, but he did what he was told. The gun slid across the hard dirt right to Ward's feet.

Ward let out a relieved sigh, then said to Meredith. "I want you to lean down very slowly and pick it up. Understand?''

Meredith kept her eyes on Travis. What did he want her to do? But he wouldn't look at her. His full attention remained on Ward.

Ward fisted his hand in her hair and yanked her back against his chest. "Understand!''

"Yes,'' she said.

He used her body as a shield as they squatted slowly toward the dirt. He kept his fingers wrapped around her hair, forcing her head back. Unable to lean forward, she patted the dirt until her fingers brushed the cold metal of the gun barrel, and then the wooden handle. She tightened her grip around the handle. Once he got the gun, he'd shoot Travis and the others.

"Easy," Ward soothed.

She tightened her grip around the handle. She'd never let Ward shoot Travis. Never.

Her gaze locked on Travis for the first time. *I'll die for you.*

His eyes shouted a silent warning. *No!*

Ward held her hair firmly. "I am a step ahead of you, Mrs. Carter. I wouldn't try anything so foolish."

In that moment, Sheriff Harper started to stir. He moaned and rolled onto his back.

The distraction was for only an instant, but it was enough. Ward whirled toward the sheriff. But before he could fire, Travis reached inside his collar and, from a small pocket, pulled the pearl-handled knife. In one fluid motion, Travis hurled the knife at Ward and struck him in the heart.

Ward stared wide-eyed at Travis, as if he couldn't quite believe what had happened. Then he dropped to his knees, pulling Meredith with him. He released her and fell back into the dirt. He stared sightlessly into the early morning sky, dead.

Travis closed the distance between him and Meredith in two strides. He pulled her to her feet and hugged her against his chest. "I thought I had lost you. I never meant for it to be so close."

She gripped handfuls of his shirt. "I was so scared."

"I was always close. Never far."

She looked down at Ward's lifeless body. "Did you hear what he said? He betrayed the prisoners."

"I heard every word. So did those two witnesses."

Sheriff Harper groaned louder. The two soldiers helped him and the other guard to their feet. "Damn, I wasn't counting on that fool hitting me so hard."

With Travis at her side Meredith went to him. She inspected the wound. "It's going to take a stitch or two."

"Reckon if my head weren't so hard, it would have been worse."

Meredith cupped the old sheriff's face. "What on earth were you doing outside?"

Sheriff Harper grinned, nodding to the young lieutenant who'd been guarding the jail. "I woke him up about an hour ago, right after Travis slipped out of the jail. The young fellow was half out of his mind with worry because he thought he'd fallen asleep on guard duty.'' He winked at Travis. ''I calmed him down and offered to stand by him and keep him up. I figured once Travis set the trap for Ward we'd get a visit sooner or later from him, but I wasn't counting on him hitting quite so hard.''

Meredith looked at the dead man. A shudder passed through her body.

Travis scowled. ''Get him out of my sight.''

The guards dragged him away.

Meredith's shoulders slumped. ''The nightmare is over.''

Travis kissed her forehead. ''We're done with worrying about the past. Will you be all right for a minute? I've got to clean up a few loose ends.''

''I'll be fine.''

She reached in her pocket, pulled out a clean cloth and pressed it to the wound on Sheriff Harper's head as Travis spoke to the other soldiers.

Travis was clearly in charge. The soldiers seemed only too happy to follow his orders. After firing off a battery of orders, he cut away from the crowd and returned toward her. His steps were sure, purposeful.

He hesitated in front of her only an instant before he opened his arms to her. She gladly went to him.

Travis held her close. "That was too damn close for me."

She savored the beat of his heart against her cheek, the warmth of his body. "What's going to happen now?"

"We still have go back to Washington. There'll be an inquiry, but with the soldiers' testimony, it's only a formality."

She swallowed. "I'm so glad it's over."

He pulled her away from him and stared into her eyes. "There's something I should have said to you last night and didn't." He laid his hands on her shoulders. "I love you, Meredith. I have from the moment you walked into Libby Prison. I wanted to touch you so much that night, but then I saw the wedding band on your finger and knew you belonged to someone else."

Tears filled her eyes and streamed down her face. "Travis." Her voice was little more than a hoarse whisper.

With his knuckle he swiped a tear away. "I know you've been through a lot of emotions these last couple of weeks. It's all moved so fast for you."

She opened her mouth to speak, but he laid his fingertips on her mouth. "We can live anywhere you want. There's a command post waiting for me—I still have a year of service left, but if you want, we can make Trail's End our home one day."

She captured his fingers in her hands. "Travis, I don't care where I live."

He swallowed. "Then you'll stay with me."

A warm smile curved the edges of her lips and she took his hands in hers. "I love you too much not to."

Travis let out a loud whoop and scooped her up in his arms. "Angel, we're gonna have a great life."

Epilogue

Meredith stood in the warm morning sun, her hands skimming the tall Colorado grasslands. These days, with her belly so swollen, walking was difficult, so she was careful not to stray far from the other officers' wives, who'd spread a welcome picnic out for the returning soldiers.

Travis and the other men, who'd been out on patrol the last week, were returning home and she was determined to give him a proper greeting.

She raised the handful of wildflowers to her nose. As far as she could see, the rich, green land stretched out before her. Above, the blue sky glistened.

Travis was close. She knew it and she was filled with a sense of peace.

Last week, she and Travis had celebrated their

first anniversary on the day that he had ridden off to complete his last assignment for the army. After twenty years of service, he'd decided to resign from the army. Once the baby was born, they were returning to Trail's End to start their new life.

Her stomach cramped and she pressed her hand into the small of her back. Their unborn child had made his intentions clear all morning and most of last night—he wanted to come into the world.

Meredith shifted uneasily. She tried to take comfort in that this would be the last time she'd have to worry about the dangers of patrol.

Another contraction gripped her belly and it took several deep breaths before she could stand straight again. "Hold on, little fellow. Wait until your daddy gets here."

Then in the distance she saw the plume of dust and heard the thud of horses hooves. The men were returning!

The wives and children gathered in a cluster, waiting. The children giggled and ran about, unaware that their mothers had slipped into an uneasy silence as the men grew closer and closer. Like her, each prayed for her husband's safe return.

Meredith spotted Travis immediately. Clutching her belly with one hand, she waved with the other. Travis waved back.

He sat straight and tall in his saddle. His hat, rimmed in gold braid, shadowed his eyes, but she could see that he was smiling. His blue jacket was covered in dust, his brass buttons tarnished, but he looked fit as did the other men.

Meredith released a sigh of relief.

Travis stayed with his men until they all reached the compound, and then he dismounted quickly. He broke away from the others and strode toward Meredith. The laugh lines at his temples were creased, his stunning blue eyes bright.

Her heart tripped. Lord, but he was a fine-looking man. "Welcome home, Major Rafferty."

He scooped her in his arms and kissed her. The kiss lingered and she savored the taste of him. His scent, a mixture of leather and fresh air, enveloped her. "Good to be home, Mrs. Rafferty."

The baby kicked hard in her stomach and thumped against Travis. He slid his hand to her belly, his face full of concern. "How are you doing?"

Before she could answer, another contraction

tightened around her like a vise. Her skin paled and for a moment she couldn't breathe.

When the pain passed, she managed a smile. "We're good."

Travis frowned. He started toward the compound and their small house. "How long has this been going on?"

"On and off for a few hours."

His jaw set with worry. "Translation—for at least a day or two. You should be in bed."

"I'm fine."

"You're not fine. You're having a baby."

Travis barked out orders as they strode into camp. Within minutes, he had the fort doctor and three women on hand next to Meredith's bedside.

As she bored down, through another pain, Travis tossed his hat aside and took her hand. He looked pale.

"You're not going to faint on me, are you?" she asked. Despite her efforts, her voice echoed her pain.

He squeezed her hand tighter. His face was as pale as she'd ever seen it. "No, but I have a lot more pity for Nathan Miller than I ever did. Let's hope I don't faint on you."

Less than an hour later, James Ezra Rafferty

was born. He weighed close to ten pounds and was gifted with a hearty set of lungs.

Meredith came through the delivery fine and Travis didn't faint.

*   *   *   *   *

MARY BURTON

calls Richmond, Virginia, home where she
lives with her husband and two children.
Rafferty's Bride is her fifth historical romance.

On the lookout for captivating courtships
set on the American frontier?
Then behold these rollicking romances
from Harlequin Historicals.

On sale January 2003

THE FORBIDDEN BRIDE
by Cheryl Reavis
Will a well-to-do young woman defy
her father and give her heart to
a wild and daring gold miner?

HALLIE'S HERO
by Nicole Foster
A beautiful rancher joins forces
with a gun-toting gambler to save her spread!

On sale February 2003

THE MIDWIFE'S SECRET
by Kate Bridges
Can a wary midwife finally find love and acceptance
in the arms of a ruggedly handsome sawmill owner?

THE LAW AND KATE MALONE
by Charlene Sands
A stubborn sheriff and a spirited saloon owner
share a stormy reunion!

 Harlequin Historicals®
Historical Romantic Adventure!

These are the stories you've been waiting for!

Based on the Harlequin Books miniseries
The Carradignes: American Royalty comes

HEIR TO THE THRONE

Brand-new stories from

KASEY MICHAELS

CAROLYN DAVIDSON

Travel to the opulent world of royalty with these two
stories that bring to readers the concluding chapters in
the quest for a ruler for the fictional country of Korosol.

Available in December 2002 at your favorite retail outlet.

HARLEQUIN®
Makes any time special®

COMING NEXT MONTH FROM

HARLEQUIN HISTORICALS®

- **BOUNTY HUNTER'S BRIDE**
  by **Carol Finch,** author of CALL OF THE WHITE WOLF
  In order to gain control over her life, a daring debutante leaves her
  fiancé at the altar and, instead, enters a marriage of convenience
  with a bounty hunter bent on vengeance! But when she does the
  unthinkable and falls in love with her husband, will pride prevent
  her from changing a temporary bargain into a permanent union?
  HH #635 ISBN# 29235-X $5.25 U.S./$6.25 CAN.

- **BADLANDS HEART**
  by **Ruth Langan,** final book in the *Badlands* series
  Kitty Conover knows a thing or two about breaking mustangs,
  but she doesn't know the first thing about love…until Bo Chandler
  comes to town. When another man claims Bo's identity, what will
  Kitty believe—the hard evidence or her heart?
  HH #636 ISBN# 29236-8 $5.25 U.S./$6.25 CAN.

- **NORWYCK'S LADY**
  by **Margo Maguire,** second in the *Widower* series
  After an embittered lord rescues a young noblewoman from
  a shipwreck, he discovers that she's lost her memory. While
  nursing the mysterious beauty back to health, he searches for her
  identity and soon discovers that she's the daughter of his most
  hated enemy.…
  HH #637 ISBN# 29237-6 $5.25 U.S./$6.25 CAN.

- **LORD SEBASTIAN'S WIFE**
  by **Katy Cooper,** author of PRINCE OF HEARTS
  A world-weary nobleman is on the verge of matrimony when the
  past comes back to haunt him. A reckless pledge made years ago will
  now bind him to a desirable, but deceptive woman!
  HH #638 ISBN# 29238-4 $5.25 U.S./$6.25 CAN.

KEEP AN EYE OUT FOR ALL FOUR
OF THESE TERRIFIC NEW TITLES

HHIBC631